This edition offers everything needed by the newcomer to this famous but intimidating text: images, maps, footnotes, and introductory essays by eighteen leading Joyceans.

James Joyce

THE CAMBRIDGE CENTENARY

ULYSSES

The 1922 Text with Essays and Notes

Edited by CATHERINE FLYNN

The Cambridge Centenary Ulysses is a brave and timely attempt to banish many of the fears that Joyce's masterpiece causes for the 'ordinary' reader, if such a being exists—Joyce didn't think so. Catherine Flynn and her team have done a welcome service of elucidation. And of course it's a great pleasure to have the facsimile of the original text.

John Banville

Save 20% with code: CCU20
www.cambridge.org/CCUlysses

9781316515945 | Hardback
June 2022 | £30 | $39.95

CAMBRIDGE
UNIVERSITY PRESS

GRANTA

12 Addison Avenue, London W11 4QR | email: editorial@granta.com
To subscribe visit subscribe.granta.com, or call +44 (0)1371 851873

ISSUE 159: SPRING 2022

This selection copyright © 2022 Granta Trust.

Granta, ISSN 173231 (USPS 508), is published four times a year by Granta Trust, 12 Addison Avenue, London W11 4QR, United Kingdom.

The US annual subscription price is $50. Airfreight and mailing in the USA by agent named World Container Inc., 150–15, 183rd Street, Jamaica, NY 11434, USA. Periodicals postage paid at Brooklyn, NY 11256.

US Postmaster: Send address changes to *Granta*, World Container Inc., 150–15, 183rd Street, Jamaica, NY 11434, USA.

Subscription records are maintained at *Granta*, c/o ESco Business Services Ltd, Wethersfield, Essex, CM7 4AY.

Air Business Ltd is acting as our mailing agent.

Granta is printed and bound in Italy by Legoprint. This magazine is printed on paper that fulfils the criteria for 'Paper for permanent document' according to ISO 9706 and the American Library Standard ANSI/NIZO Z39.48-1992 and has been certified by the Forest Stewardship Council (FSC). *Granta* is indexed in the American Humanities Index.

ISBN 978-1-909-889-47-7

**Edinburgh
International
Book Festival**

13–29 August
2022

The World, in Words

Come together for over 500 events
featuring the best writers from around
the world. Enjoy summer days in our
new home at Edinburgh College of Art,
or join in the discussion online.

**Programme launch: early June
Tickets on sale in late June**

edbookfest.co.uk | @edbookfest

The Bell Jar

SYLVIA PLATH

Introduced by
HEATHER CLARK

Illustrations by
ALEXANDRA LEVASSEUR

'I was supposed to be
having the time of my life.'

Esther Greenwood, *The Bell Jar*

The Folio Society

Exclusively available from
FOLIOSOCIETY.COM

CONTENTS

SUZIE HOWELL
Sizewell B, for *Granta*, 2022

ON SIZEWELL C

William Atkins

There are places, even in temperate England, where a lack and an excess of water meet, shaping the landscape as surely as the grinding of tectonic plates. The belt of heath known as the Sandlings, on the Suffolk coast between Aldeburgh and Great Yarmouth, lies in one of the driest parts of the country. The low rainfall, about half the national average, is felt keenly by farmers, who must also cope with fast-draining sandy soils. Although the Sandlings was historically relegated to the grazing of sheep, which can make do with dew and grass for long periods, intensive irrigation means that today vegetables can thrive here. In summer, the pulsing silver arcs of spraying machines lend perspective to the flat landscape, their twenty-metre jets casting back and forth over fields of potatoes or onions.

But the history of water in this part of eastern England is not only one of want; the region is also defined by inundation. To look out to sea – it might be from the beach at Sizewell – is to look upon a drowned realm: from time to time, fishing boats will dredge up spearheads or mammoth teeth from the area known as Doggerland, which until the sea rose around 6500 BC connected Britain to mainland Europe. There are more recent losses. The best-known local story of inundation is that of Dunwich, the medieval port and religious centre destroyed by the sea over the course of centuries.

Today, little more hangs on than a row of houses and the ruins of the thirteenth-century friary. The sea's work continues. Locals tend to give the gravelly cliffs a wide berth when walking on the beach.

Five miles south of Dunwich, on the edge of the Sandlings, is Leiston, 'a little northern mill town dumped in the middle of Suffolk', as one long-term resident described it to me. Its industrial heritage makes it unusual in a region still dominated by farming. It was out of the land that Leiston's industry emerged, with the founding in 1778 of the Richard Garrett and Sons engineering works, a small manufacturer of agricultural tools – scythes, sickles and later mechanical chaff-cutters – which grew over the course of a century and more to become a world-leading producer of steam engines, trolleybuses and industrial boilers. In 1852 the Long Shop, a cavernous hall with an internal gallery, was built in the centre of Leiston for building portable steam engines, one of the world's first assembly lines. You would find Garrett's machines (and Garrett's sales reps) everywhere, from Patagonia and Siberia to the peat bogs of Ireland. Until the mid-twentieth century, when Garrett's entered its decline, Leiston was essentially a company town. Well into the 1970s the firm employed up to 600 people in a town whose population in 1971 was 4,790. Even Leiston's domestic water was supplied by Garrett's until the First World War. After the war, the firm's fortunes waned; its slow decline, marked by a failure to adapt to modern production methods, culminated in asset-stripping and mass redundancies in the late 1970s and finally closure in 1980. It is in this sense that Leiston can be said to resemble a northern mill town – it is a place with a powerful void at its centre, haunted by bygone affluence, but whose sense of community is no less real for being vestigial.

Today, the renovated Long Shop forms part of a museum. In an adjoining hall stand a horse-drawn clover huller, and a seed drill and a thresher, both of the latter steam-driven via belts; in another room is an industrial steam boiler from the 1970s: 'A boiler/steam generator is a device used to create steam by applying heat energy to water,' reads the sign.

Climb the stairs to the wooden gallery of the Long Shop and, in an uncharacteristically neglected corner, you will find a model of another kind of steam generator: under dusty glass, a maquette of Sizewell B nuclear power station with its distinctive white reactor Dome, which was displayed at the 1983 public inquiry into the proposed development. Some of the model trees have crumbled. Nearby is a poster showing how a pressurised-water reactor works, with its three circuits: one passing pressurised water through the reactor vessel, a second passing steam through the turbines to create electricity, and a third bringing cooling water from the sea to condense that steam back into water. The two crucial substances, it is apparent, are uranium and water.

V iewed from a fishing boat off the hamlet of Sizewell, two miles east of Leiston, the reactor Dome stands alongside the low blue hangar of Sizewell B's turbine hall and, to the south, the corrugated grey blocks of Sizewell A's now inactive reactor building and turbine hall.

East Suffolk's flatness means that such tall structures are visible for many miles, even on land. It often looks as if the two stations are one, the 65-metre-tall Dome of Sizewell B seeming to emerge from the cuboids of the decommissioned Sizewell A, though more than 300 metres separate the two. I've seen the Dome – my instinct is to capitalise it – from as far away as Southwold nine miles to the north and the old military testing site at Orford Ness nine miles to the south, and it is frequently sighted unexpectedly from far inland, rising like a moon above a line of trees or under a bank of cloud. Viewed from a low hill near my home in the village of Westleton – a Suffolk mountain, this hill, at twenty metres above sea level – the Dome four miles away shifts in colour throughout the day, and from one day to the next, sometimes appearing as transparent as a contact lens, sometimes solid rose or pale blue, sometimes sunlit white against dark sea-clouds. Its apparent size and proximity, too, vary with the conditions: one day it will seem far more distant than four miles, a foreign dot on the horizon; the next, it is as much a part of the spirit of the place as the line of holm oaks or the thatched church in the village below. At night it glows beneath a yellowish haze.

From out at sea, the Dome dominates the coastline. The boat's skipper, Noel Cattermole, is the only commercial inshore fisherman between Aldeburgh and Southwold, a stretch that was once dominated by fishing. He is one of those people in rural England, like the publican, the parish councillor or the cannabis dealer, who earn a certain kind of local fame. Everyone seems to know him. His stock-in-trade: rock eel, bass, the tenderest Dover sole you will ever eat. In summer there are crabs and lobsters being sluiced out in a tub behind his gutting counter. He's meaning to retire, but he still goes out most mornings.

'That's my son,' he says, when I ask about the boat's name. The *Joseph William* is a 22-foot longshore beach boat with a dark blue fibreglass hull and an iroko-wood gunnel patinaed from fifteen years' near-daily use. The floor is crammed with plastic crates overflowing with nets. We move north, engine churning, from Sizewell village, with its single line of houses, between the beach and the submerged ridge of sediment known as the Sizewell Bank. Cormorants rise, one by one, from the rusting iron outfall headworks of Sizewell A, its girders lined with disused kittiwake nests like teacups on a dresser. The station stopped operating in 2006 but the site is not expected to be fully cleared and decontaminated for nearly another eighty years. We circle a wooden stanchion 600 metres out that marks the seawater intake for Sizewell B, the surface giving no hint of what is happening below us, the millions of litres of water per minute being sucked into the station's cooling system through two giant tunnels.

If you take the public tour of Sizewell B, they tell you proudly that the Dome is bigger than that of St Paul's Cathedral. But while the impression from any distance is religious, at first sight it is a mosque that Sizewell B suggests: the white of the Dome and the blue of the turbine hall; the broad and low proportions of the latter, like a prayer hall; and the tile-like cladding covering it all. The hulks of Sizewell A, next door, are a franker, more uncompromising presence. In *The*

Rings of Saturn, as W.G. Sebald plods over Dunwich Heath, he sees the reactor building three miles south as a 'glowering mausoleum'. A towering concrete block, like a vast windowless car park, it is more explicitly industrial than its successor. But it is the Dome of B that bears the symbolic burden: it has the function of an emblem, but what precisely that emblem signifies is complex and contested. When I first moved here – when the whole place was strange and I hardly knew north from south – it seemed as sinister, in the secrecy of its form, as an alien vessel or a giant egg erupted from the soil. But like any familiar landmark, after a while you come to regard it with something like affection, even if you recognise it for what it is: a blight.

'There,' says Noel, pointing to a rise of scrubland immediately to its north: 'that's where it'll start.'

I send my partner a photo and she texts: 'Like approaching Istanbul across the Bosporus!'

And it's true. You can imagine, as you head shoreward, that you are coming into an ancient city, having travelled a great distance.

A certain rigour in Noel's gait, even when we get back to his yard, suggests he is moving against a gradient. He doesn't like to be too far from the beach, especially when he is on land. A modestly proprietorial presence in Sizewell village, he is usually found, when not at sea, in the yard next to his house on Sizewell's front, from which he sells his catch direct, or on the beach attending to the *Joseph William*, or at the cafe, Sizewell Tea, which is run by his son.

Having lived here for more than fifty years, Noel has a unique relationship with the nuclear site. He was eleven when his family moved to the hamlet from a village eight miles inland, well outside the Sandlings. In those days there were half a dozen boats working off this beach. 'I took my O levels and next day I started fishing. And that's all I've ever done.' Sitting in his kitchen, divested of his bib-and-braces, he reflects on recent events in the tone of someone expressing a conclusion he has reached only gradually and with reluctance.

'I've got no axe to grind, but I do find that anti-nuclear people can be very *aggressive*.'

On a Sunday morning a few weeks earlier, the plain of rabbit-grazed grassland between the dunes and Sizewell B had filled with people. The dominant colours were the fluorescent yellow of the tabards the 600 participants had been asked to wear, and the red and yellow of the STOP SIZEWELL C logo, on flags and banners, which by now was familiar to anyone who lived in the area. Stepping between the crowd's legs, a beautiful black whippet carried the same words on a sheet of paper ribboned to its flank. I watched the crowd gather from the top of a dune: the snaking line of DayGlo yellow bodies; the white of the Dome; the blue of the sky. The atmosphere didn't really seem aggressive. Occasionally someone would slip from the line and dash over the dunes for a hidden pee, but before rejoining the hubbub they would halt for a moment to gaze out at the crashing waves. Even more than usual, the line of dunes marked the boundary between two worlds.

Before the end of the current parliament, in 2024, the government has pledged to approve funding for at least one new nuclear power station. It is an arresting fact that all of Britain's eight functioning nuclear power stations are owned by the same company, EDF Energy, a subsidiary of Électricité de France, which in turn is majority owned by the French state. Although it has a monopoly on electricity production in France, EDF's financial position has been precarious since the 2008 crash, and it declined further after the disaster at Fukushima, the Japanese nuclear power station that in 2011 was catastrophically damaged, releasing radioactivity into the atmosphere, as a consequence of the Tohoku earthquake and tsunami. Last year, EDF's debt rose to £34 billion, while its share price has almost halved in the past three years. Its CEO has admitted that without the UK, its most important export market, the nuclear industry in France would cease to be sustainable. In 2012, after a National Policy Statement for Nuclear Power identified eight sites in England and Wales, including Sizewell, where new nuclear power stations could be deployed by 2025, EDF submitted a proposal to build a pair of European pressurised-water reactors (EPR) alongside Sizewell B, which is due to be decommissioned no earlier than 2035.

The centrepiece of EDF's export strategy, the EPR is a powerful advanced version of the standard pressurised-water reactor operating at Sizewell B, and in principle safer and more efficient. Of the four others in the world, however, only a pair at Taishan, China, has ever been commercially operative, and one of them was shut down in June 2021 due to a cracked fuel rod. The Olkiluoto 3 EPR in Finland was turned on in December 2021 after a twelve-year delay, but has yet to be connected to the national grid. In *The Fall and Rise of Nuclear Power in Britain* (2016), Simon Taylor describes the EPR as 'one of the most complex objects ever built', while Dr Paul Dorfman of UCL's Energy Institute, interviewed in a documentary about EDF's woes (*The French Nuclear Trap*, 2019), calls the EPR a 'failed reactor', which is 'too complex to build on time or to cost'. Two are currently under construction by EDF at Hinkley Point C in Somerset, Britain's first new nuclear power station since Sizewell B in 1995. It is running ten years late and at least £1.5 billion overbudget. The model for that project, EDF's Flamanville 3, in France, is more than nine years late. The model for Sizewell C is to be Hinkley Point C.

In May 2020 EDF submitted its application for development consent to the government. By the company's own reckoning, Sizewell C, which was to be part-funded by the state-owned China General Nuclear Power Group (CGN), would take up to twelve years to build, at a cost of £20 billion. A new bypass, link roads and roundabout would be needed for the 700 heavy-goods vehicles that would attend the construction zone each day, as well as a temporary railway extension, a loading jetty, and a campus to accommodate up to 2,400 of a peak workforce of nearly 8,000 (almost twice the population of Leiston). Almost 1,380 acres of the Sandlings and the surrounding countryside would be engulfed by the construction site, including a Site of Special Scientific Interest, while spoil heaps and cranes would be visible for miles.

Opponents say it would be a crime to build a third nuclear power station on this famously eroding coast. You only need to consider the North Sea Flood of 1953, which inundated the east coast, Scotland, the Netherlands and parts of Belgium, or for that matter Fukushima, whose backup generators failed after the site was flooded by a tsunami. A map produced by the US-based science journalism organisation Climate Central, marking land that is projected to be below annual flood level in 2050, shows EDF's site largely surrounded by water, a nuclear island. Sizewell C, if it goes ahead, will operate until at least 2095 and take decades to decommission. Some of its stockpile of thousands of tonnes of spent fuel, meanwhile, will remain hazardously radioactive for hundreds of thousands of years. Currently every pellet from Sizewell B's spent assemblies is being stored onsite, in either cooling ponds or sealed canisters, with no plan for their removal.

In autumn 2021, as the protest took place at Sizewell, the six-month public examination into EDF's application was nearing its end, leaving the five-person examining authority to consider its findings and make its recommendation to the Secretary of State for Business, Energy and Industrial Strategy. EDF says Sizewell C will 'save 9 million tonnes of CO_2 emissions every year' and that without nuclear power Britain will be unable to meet its commitment to reduce its carbon emissions by 100 per cent by 2050 ('net zero'). Sizewell C, it says, will generate thousands of short- and long-term jobs and invest millions into the local economy. (In 2020, a new claim appeared in EDF's regular community newsletter, posted through the door of local homes: 'The project will be a welcome boost to the recovery of the East Anglian economy as we emerge from the Coronavirus pandemic.') The company notes that the coastline at Sizewell has been relatively stable over the past 200 years, and insists the site will be protected from worst-case-scenario sea-level rises and storm surges. Indeed, the purpose of the protest that day was not to draw attention to the risk of inundation but to highlight the extent of the foreshore that would be obliterated by EDF's planned coastal defences.

Participants were instructed to spread out along a line that marked the seaward perimeter of a massive revetment that would bury more than a square mile of the dunes and grassland under up to fourteen metres of rock, concrete and soil. Even in the sunshine it was possible to imagine the mass of earthworks towering over your head. But the mood that morning had not been gloomy; there were children playing tag and people who knew each other from yoga, and a few cheerful veterans from the campaign against Sizewell B.

'I've seen all this with B,' says Noel, who has been fishing off Sizewell since there was just one power station here. 'All the same scenario.'

Press photos from a 1986 anti-Sizewell B march, which drew more than a thousand protesters to the village, suggest something more in keeping with the unionised industrial rallies of the time. Greenpeace activists in inflatable boats attached a banner to the outfall rig, reading VOTE OUT NUCLEAR POWER, and the Campaign for Nuclear Disarmament logo was ubiquitous. Postcards had been printed referencing a Ukrainian town nobody had heard of until six months earlier: SIZEWELL – TWINNED WITH CHERNOBYL. The global implications of that disaster were still emerging.

Noel had been more sympathetic back then. 'We didn't know what to think, really. It was a lot bigger than Sizewell A. But we went with it. And at the end of the day, yes we had a few problems. But you have to have something going on, on this island, don't you? Some industry.'

The three groups that organised last week's event, Stop Sizewell C, Together Against Sizewell C and Suffolk Coastal Friends of the Earth, had arranged overflow parking outside the village, and in emails urged participants to avoid trampling the delicate flora of the foreshore; but Noel felt overwhelmed. Inconsiderate parking was one thing; more objectionable was what seemed to him a sort of righteous sanctimony. 'They were offhand, shall we say.'

Sizewell A was already there, newly operational, when he arrived as a boy; he watched as B was approved and slowly went up. Sizewell itself, he maintains, was not massively affected by the influx of temporary construction workers, even if Leiston, where many of them were billeted, was another matter. 'They want women, they want drink and they want betting shops.' (An insistent rumour has it that sex workers were bussed in from Lowestoft.) The one thing Noel regretted, 'my biggest loss', was that the marsh nearby, which had been leased historically to Leiston and District Wildfowlers Association, was handed to the adjoining RSPB Minsmere reserve, meaning he could no longer shoot there. He still likes to go out with his gun and his Labrador. The type who recoils at country sports is the same type, it seems to him, who banned the culling of seals (which take fish from his nets) and imposed quotas that make it virtually impossible for a lone fisherman to earn a living. 'It's all conservation, now. They want me in a picture postcard, but they don't want me catching fish.' He remembers a time when seals would vanish when they saw his boat; now they swim up to it.

Sometimes you'd think nuclear fission were an activity as indigenous to the area as growing beet or catching herring. At the launch of a public inquiry into a proposal for a gas-cooled nuclear-power station at Trawsfynydd, Wales, as long ago as 1958, objectors were outnumbered by people waving banners reading PYLONS BEFORE POVERTY. The slogans haven't changed much. Addressing a Westminster Environment, Energy and Transport Forum in January 2021, Sizewell C's Director of Financing showed a slide of one of Stop Sizewell C's banners. It had been defaced, using spray paint, with what she told the audience was 'a piece of quite nicely rhyming graffiti', which apparently encapsulated 'a lot of the debate about Sizewell C': JOBS NOT SNOBS.

Because Noel lives closer to the site than almost anyone, opponents of Sizewell C do tend to expect him to be an ally. 'I might not say what you want me to say,' he had warned me – but he could only speak as he found, even if some people didn't like it. 'They'll say I'm irresponsible, ill-educated, bought-off; whatever. Whatever.' But the people up at the station, whether they were the Central Electricity Generating Board (CEGB), Nuclear Electric, British Energy or, now, EDF, have usually listened to him if he has any concerns.

The armed Civil Nuclear Constabulary officers who patrol the beach 24/7 mean there is virtually no crime, and scientists come round every couple of months to test his catch and pass a Geiger counter over his lobster pots. Households within a kilometre of the site are issued with stable-iodine tablets to be taken in the event of a leak, to prevent the body absorbing radiation. But you learn not to worry. If and when C happens, he expects to be compensated for any temporary limitation to his fishing grounds, just as he was when B was built.

'It's still a wonderful place to live. I wouldn't want to live anywhere else.' The protesters were a bit like dinner guests who told you your neighbourhood was going to the dogs. 'It's quite strange when people have moved to this area in the last ten years, people with money, people who could afford to buy a house anywhere in the country . . . You've already got A and B here. If this is such a shit area, why would somebody with all that money move here? Sizewell C has been coming ever since Sizewell B was finished.'

You could say it has been coming even longer. On the 1904 Ordnance Survey map, Sizewell is separated from industrial Leiston by a couple of miles of heathland: an isolated spot in an isolated part of a county itself long considered an English hinterland, despite its proximity to London, eighty miles to the south.

The closeness of the two settlements is suggested by the administrative name of the town council: Leiston-cum-Sizewell. Published for holidaymakers in 1935, the *Official Guide to Leiston* boasts of 'efficient public services' and a 'pure and abundant' water supply, a significant virtue, at the time, in England's driest region. The guide goes on to extol the 'lovely gorse-clad heathlands stretching eastward to the sand dunes and beaches on the seaboard at Sizewell', and a photo shows a host of children playing among dunes.

In 1957, a 32-year-old bird enthusiast named Michael Gammon came here as part of a tour of the Suffolk coast. He would have found the region interesting on account of RSPB Minsmere, opened ten years earlier, where rare avocets had recently started breeding.

But Gammon, a nuclear engineer, had been sent on a quest by his employer, the Central Electricity Generating Board, Britain's nationalised electricity generator, to select a site for a new gas-cooled Magnox nuclear power station, one of eight commissioned in England and Wales over the next nine years. The explicit motivation for this massive investment in nuclear power was a combination of anxiety about domestic coal shortages and, more immediately, the 1956 Suez Crisis, which had highlighted the vulnerability of global oil supplies.

Seven spots along a 22-mile stretch of Suffolk coast were considered by Gammon, including Sizewell. If you examine a map of UK nuclear power stations, you'll see that almost without exception they are sited on the coast (the exception is Trawsfynydd, which stands beside a reservoir). The main reason for this coastal clustering is that a large body of deep water is needed for the station's cooling system. But there is another advantage: if the worst happens, 180 degrees around the site will, for some distance, by definition be free of any dwelling. These are the two factors nuclear developers must reconcile: for safety reasons, population limits are imposed upon the surrounding area; at the same time, a station must be close enough to population centres for the efficient transfer of electricity. The Suffolk coast, then, appealed to Gammon and the CEGB partly for the same reasons it appeals to the thousands of second-homers who travel here from London for the weekend – remote but not too remote, sparsely populated and near the sea. The spot he settled upon consisted, in his words, of 'low-grade agricultural and heathland, with three small woods, mainly on a low plateau above flood level'.

A letter from Leiston town council to the Ministry of Power in 1957 expressed qualified enthusiasm for the project. More impassioned is a letter held in the National Archives from a local resident, Mr Kelly: 'I want to tell you personally, as a private person, how desperately our people are hoping this project may be realised. If, as we hope and pray, it may be realised, a heavy cloud will be lifted, and our morale will soar.' This was at a time when Garrett's fortunes were diminishing: there had been lay-offs, overtime had been cancelled and the factory was considering imposing a four-day week. If the power station did not go ahead, Mr Kelly added, 'it would be hard to see anything to which we could fasten our hopes of improvement.'

When the proposal was announced in the local press in January 1959, only nine objections were raised. 'The station will make no smoke and leave no ash,' one paper assured its readers later that year. The CEGB was confident that a public inquiry would be pointless. 'It seems unlikely that anyone would appear to state any reasoned case against it.' But even Michael Gammon and the Ministry of Power were surprised when East Suffolk County Planning Committee took the same position, and in February 1960, with virtually no public scrutiny, gave the project its approval. Three years later, the *Suffolk Mercury* celebrated the completion of the cooling-water intake: 'Woman councillor goes through under-sea tunnel at Sizewell'. Mrs Reade, it went on, 'had to complete the journey on her hands and knees'.

T he prospect of Sizewell C revived a despair Joan Girling, a former Labour councillor, has known all her life. 'The government wants it. The district council wants it. The county council – they'll follow the district, because they haven't got enough teeth. And they're all Conservative-led anyway. I'm terrified.'

We are sitting on a bench above Sizewell beach, looking out to the 1960s intake headworks and the waters where Noel fishes, our backs to the silent mountain of Sizewell A. Summer is almost over, and it is not warm, but the undulating grasslands between here and the beach, known locally as the benthills, are scattered with colour: yellow horned poppy, silver-blue sea holly, clusters of blue harebells dancing in the breeze. When Joan was brought here for the first time, on a school trip shortly before Sizewell A was approved in 1960, it seemed perfect to her, actually perfect.

To say the hamlet is overshadowed by the power stations is not quite right: from the beach, A is partly screened by a remnant of the woods Gammon mentioned, and B is in turn screened by A. Perhaps this contributes to Noel's ambivalence: from his yard you are barely aware of the power stations; it's only when you look back from any distance that they rise up, the discrepancy in scale making the village seem like an Everest base camp.

Joan's life has been shaped by the CEGB's decision to put a nuclear power station here in 1959. When she was a girl she lived in an isolated pair of cottages on a T-junction in nearby Darsham, her grandmother in one, Joan and her parents in the other. 'Dad had a letter to say that because they were building a nuclear power plant, they wanted to cut the front off the garden.' Dozens of buses per day would be bringing construction workers to Sizewell from Halesworth, and the junction needed to be 'splayed' to improve visibility. 'Dad's bristles went up: "I'm not selling my land."' But his solicitors warned him the alternative would be compulsory purchase at a lower rate. 'And they cut the whole corner off: a big pond with a beautiful hawthorn hedge and four great big oak trees.'

Joan first lived in Leiston in 1962, after she married. Her then husband was working as a banksman, directing cranes at the Sizewell site. Seventeen years later, after her divorce, she moved with her children to a house just outside Sizewell. Eight years after that, Sizewell B was granted planning permission. Unable to face the disruption, the noise and the destruction, Joan moved once again, to a farmhouse on the outskirts of town, where she lives today. 'It's pained me all my life, the wretched thing.' She might be forgiven for feeling hounded. If Sizewell C goes ahead, EDF wants to build a railway extension that will pass 200 metres from her garden.

Joan co-founded what is now called Together Against Sizewell C (TASC) in 2008 to oppose not just Sizewell C but, according to the group's current constitution, 'all other such nuclear installations as TASC considers it necessary to oppose, and TASC will undertake all lawful activities as it sees fit in order to prevent such developments'. Its chairman is Pete Wilkinson, a co-founder of Greenpeace UK, who was involved in a famous action in 1983 to block the offshore outfall pipe at Sellafield, which was discharging radioactive waste into the Irish Sea. TASC sometimes collaborates with Stop Sizewell C, the other group dedicated to campaigning against a third power station (for example, in organising the protest at Sizewell in September), but the two have chosen not to merge. Their approaches differ.

Stop Sizewell C was founded in 2013 as the Theberton and Eastbridge Action Group, to defend the interests of the two villages likely to be most affected by Sizewell C. The group does not, significantly, describe itself as anti-nuclear and did not at first oppose the power station. It changed its stance – and thus its name – when its members found that EDF was not listening to its concerns. It has a full-time executive director (also ex-Greenpeace) and spent nearly £100,000 on campaigning in 2020. Its most visible action has been the distribution of flyers and yard signs, designed by a local ex-Saatchi creative, in red and yellow with a variety of anti-Sizewell slogans and an ominous red half-circle suggesting a reactor dome. Over the course of 2021, these signs mushroomed in the front windows, gardens and verges of the surrounding communities, albeit few were seen in Leiston or Sizewell.

Joan doesn't visit Sizewell often, any more. Too painful. She is unafraid to acknowledge that the loss of the perfect place she discovered as a teenager might represent the larger losses of her life, whatever they might be. But to object to such harms – to having your peace disturbed by freight trains, to seeing the view you love destroyed – is not sentimental or solipsistic; it is just to insist that environmental harm is an attack on the human soul. As she sees it, 'Sizewell', in whatever iteration, however it might evolve, is a single monolithic disfigurement, the ruin of all that's beautiful to her, *the wretched thing*. Shortly before we met, at the examining authority's request, EDF had produced a series of 'construction-phase visualisations', Photoshopped mock-ups of various views of Sizewell as it would appear during the up-to-twelve years of construction. The document received little public attention, but to anyone familiar with the view from Dunwich Heath or the beach at RSPB Minsmere, it was enough to make you actually gasp, so closely did it match your worst imaginings. Sizewell A and B were all but hidden by a forest of cranes, perhaps forty in all, the tallest – the world's tallest, at a quarter of a kilometre – dwarfing the Dome. Visible, too, were the spoil heaps towering over Eastbridge and the unloading jetty extending hundreds of metres into the sea. Another visualisation showed the same view at night, the tangle of cranes lit white against a yellow-stained sky. It looked like the building site for a colony on Mars.

In 1983 a fundraising gala for the campaign against the planned Sizewell B, 'Too Hot to Handle', was held at the Apollo Victoria, London. Its line-up included Madness and UB40, and a comic skit in which Michael Palin played a nuclear inspector greasing up the audience. 'We're often accused of not caring for the views of rabid, politically motivated minorities,' he said. 'But we *do* care.' The PM, he went on, had asked him to attend the event, 'in a spirit of reasonableness and cooperation, to talk to you about . . . Sizewell *H*. It seems inconceivable,' he continued, 'that back in 1983 there were people who said we shouldn't build Sizewell *B*!'

Sir Frank Layfield QC, the planning inspector who led the Sizewell B public inquiry that had begun earlier that year, recognised the development's sublime ugliness long before it existed, concluding that 'the new station would be a totally inappropriate intrusion into the Suffolk countryside. Its vast, featureless bulk means that it is unlikely to become accepted with time, as have other industrial buildings in rural areas.' So detrimental would be the 'visual effect of Sizewell B on the local landscape . . . that unless the proposal is held to be justified in the national interest, consent and permission should be refused'.

The national-interest argument was powerful, in the view of the CEGB and the government, particularly following the fluctuations in oil prices prompted by the OPEC crisis of 1973 and the Iranian Revolution of 1979. There were also the miners. As the historian of nuclear power Simon Taylor puts it: 'The Conservatives were instinctively pro-nuclear, partly because they were anti-coal.'

Six miles from Sizewell, on the edge of the reedbeds of the River Alde, stands another of those industrial buildings in a rural area, Snape Maltings. The hangar-like brick halls were built in the 1840s by Newson Garrett (grandson of Richard, the Leiston engineer), for malting barley for brewing. In 1967, after the site went out of use, Benjamin Britten and Peter Pears, founders of the Aldeburgh Festival, had the idea of converting the buildings into a concert venue. In the absence of other appropriate public spaces in the region, it was here that the Sizewell B public inquiry was held. It lasted for more than two years, from 11 January 1983 to 7 March 1985, the longest planning inquiry in British history at that time. At a cost of £25 million, it was also the most expensive.

Its expense and scale and frequent obscurity were not accidental. For the CEGB, and the government, it was a means of refining nuclear policy, and it was intended to be sufficiently comprehensive as to settle the whole question of nuclear power's legitimacy for the foreseeable future. In the view of Frank Layfield, the case for building Sizewell *A* had never been convincingly made. Nor, he said, did its presence alone justify the building of an adjacent successor. Without the associated electricity-transmission works, there would be few grounds to consider the CEGB's chosen site for B. It seems to have been with some sorrow that he finally approved the application to the Energy Secretary in December 1986.

An academic assessment, *Sizewell B: An Anatomy of the Inquiry* (1988), written by two environmental scientists and a lawyer, concluded that the mammoth inquiry was 'likely to be the first and last of its kind', for the simple reason that 'multinational capital tends to shy away from investing in controversial projects in Britain, when the more clinical and steady French hearing or the efficient and rule-laden German models may provide more favourable investment opportunities'. What was more, 'big inquiries also annoy, embarrass and, at times, frighten governments. The modern version has a habit of getting too close to delicate policy matters.'

'There was period of time when myself, my brother and one of my uncles were on A-station.' After forty-three years, Danny Bailey was preparing to retire in March. As we spoke, his bosses were interviewing for his successor as Sizewell B maintenance manager. He was born and raised in Leiston, his grandfather was a farmworker, his father went from the land to Garrett's, which paid better, then from Garrett's to Sizewell A, soon after it opened in 1966, which was in turn better paid than Garrett's.

'He could go to the A-station and earn more as an unskilled operator than as a trained welder at Garrett's.' ('A-station'; 'B-station': the insiders' formulation.)

Danny as a boy had wanted to be a soldier, longed to join up. A physical at sixteen identified a hearing problem (he's all but deaf in that ear now), and so for a Leiston boy it was either Garrett's or Sizewell. Offered a place on both apprenticeship schemes, he chose Sizewell for the same reason as his father: good pay, relatively speaking, at a time when Garrett's was no longer a byword for secure employment, let alone a job for life.

From his office in the administration zone, we crossed into the red zone, where protective equipment must be worn, demarked by a double red//green line painted on the ground. There was a constant muffled hum, a hum rendered sinister by its muffling. The red zone, which covers thirty-two acres, is conspicuous for its lack of vegetation, a sanitation and fire-prevention measure. The only life you see, apart from the occasional boiler-suited operative crossing the thoroughfares between buildings, or one of the massive Civil Nuclear Constabulary officers with an automatic rifle, is the herring gulls: in spring they nest on the belts of gravel laid down around the buildings, and become defensive enough to make you glad of your hard hat. Otherwise it's a coldly synthetic world, like a world from a computer game. The smell that hits you as you approach the seaward perimeter, though, is definitely organic. A morgue-like reek, it emanates from the nightmare depths of a six-metre-wide well full of sloshing yellowish foam, the outfall surge-chamber, where the station's used water, millions of litres each hour, is collected before being returned to the sea.

It's surprising to turn a corner, even comforting, in this maze of concrete and steel, and see a technology apparently transplanted from a bygone rural England: a row of four waterwheels, each more than ten metres in diameter, sunk in their pits with water sheeting from their paddles as they turn. Between them and the outer perimeter, facing onto the seafront, is a forty-metre-wide embayment of unhappy brown water drawn from the offshore inlet. It is this reservoir that feeds the wheels. The set-up is designed to filter debris and particulates, anything bigger than a centimetre, from the 3 million litres of water per minute that are being removed from the sea for cooling. Buoys, nets, driftwood, pebbles, fish. The paddles on the four wheels lift anything that makes it through the intake tunnel – millions of fish per year, dozens of species – dropping them into a funnel to be delivered back to sea.

Two weeks earlier, Noel had manoeuvred the *Joseph William* towards a flurry of white birds: twenty or more herring gulls and cormorants circling and plunging into a maelstrom of brown water, water that was churning with enough energy, when we entered it, to cause the boat to yaw. A seal lifted its head. Fifteen feet down, according to the boat's digital sounding, was the mouth of Sizewell B's outfall tunnel. I saw what the gulls and seal were excited about. The water's surface was a soup of fish, all the smaller or more delicate species – mostly herring and sprat – that had been sucked into the cooling system and could not survive the journey.

A lot of the human energy expended in creating nuclear energy is associated with cleaning water. As well as seawater, a pressurised-water reactor needs large volumes of fresh water, supplied, in the case of Sizewell, from local aquifers. This water, too, is used for cooling – cooling the reactor, and almost as importantly, cooling the spent fuel once it has been removed from the reactor. While seawater for the condenser only needs to be strained of fish and particulates, water for the reactor and cooling ponds must be filtered to an extremely high standard to prevent mineral build-up. Much of Danny's working life – eight years at the radwaste facility alone – has been dedicated to monitoring and regulating the purity of water, first as it enters the station (as an engineer on the water-treatment plant), and then as it leaves (as manager of the radwaste building). The water-treatment plant, which he helped to build, purifies the region's hard, calcium-heavy mains water to a level where it can safely be passed through the reactor and circulated in the spent-fuel ponds. Then, in the radwaste building, irradiated water is cleaned to a quality sufficient, under EDF's environmental licences, for it to be discharged into the sea.

The water-treatment plant was a riddle of pipework and boilers that it was impossible, for a layperson encased in regulation protective glasses, earplugs, gloves and Covid mask, to begin to really *perceive*, let alone interpret, while the sheer noise meant that Danny's shouted efforts to penetrate my earplugs were largely lost. If Sizewell was a mystery from a distance (from sea, or from the hill near my home), it was a mystery, too, once you were in it. What I understood was that water comes in *here!*, and goes out *there!*, and in between is successively demineralised and degassed as it passes through five humming tanks, until it emerges in an almost completely pure state.

The turbine hall was worse: a cavernous gallery as big as an airship hangar, containing twin turbines the size of London buses, spinning in their cylinders at twice the speed of sound. To look up from the gantries was dizzying, to look down was dizzying, the whole experience was dizzying. Even with earplugs the volume was tremendous. By now I understood the basic engineering principles, but I could not begin to comprehend how the ranks of tanks, valves, pumps, ducts and pipes in their thousands interacted – it was like beholding an alien city, or being dropped into the howling heart of some vast spaceship's engine.

What I was left with was simply a distinct feeling of having been in proximity to *energy* in its purest form, energy of a magnitude I had been exposed to nowhere else save for the natural world at its most Romantically sublime – at sea in a gale, or on a mountain in a thunderstorm. Part of me, as I trailed after Danny along the elevated gantries, was screaming with the thrill and terror of it, and when we emerged into the daylight and could remove our earplugs and glasses, I had to collect myself: it was almost impossible to believe that such a creation existed, here, on this quiet stretch of the English coast, on the edge of drowned Doggerland.

I understood, as I had not really understood before coming here, that the Dome I knew so well stood for something extraordinary and perhaps terrible – and above all that the source of the energy, and of the vibrations that seemed to hum in my bones for hours after, was the collision of hot and cold: that is, ultimately, uranium dug from Australia and H_2O pumped from the chalk aquifers beneath our feet.

The realisation was salient because, as the planning examination into Sizewell C was nearing its end, a preoccupation of the five examiners was precisely *where* fresh water for the two reactors would come from, to say nothing of the water needed to cool the spent fuel or batch the concrete during construction. Sizewell's water supplier, confusingly, is Northumbrian Water, based nearly 220 miles away in Durham. Operating as Essex and Suffolk Water, it supplies 1,000 square miles of eastern England, divided into four water resource zones. In EDF's 2020 planning application, most of the fresh water for construction and operation was to come from the local Blyth zone, but in June Northumbrian Water had told EDF the Blyth aquifers did not contain enough water to serve Sizewell C. Sizewell B already uses about 800,000 litres of fresh water per day, while Sizewell C, with its twin reactors, is expected to use more than 2 million litres per day, and up to 3.5 million during construction. The issue was still being debated days from the end of the six-month public examination. As my guide Danny put it, speaking of Sizewell B, 'You couldn't run a nuclear reactor without clean water.'

The only recorded serious incident at Sizewell, in the nearly sixty years since A had opened, was associated with a shortage of water. One Sunday in January 2007, a pipe feeding the spent-fuel cooling pond at the part-decommissioned Sizewell A ruptured. The alarm that should have sounded failed, and potential disaster was only averted by a contractor who happened to notice a puddle of water on the floor of an adjacent laundry. According to the preliminary report of the Nuclear Installations Inspectorate (now the Office for Nuclear

Regulation): 'the pond would have drained down in ten hours and there would have arisen a very significant risk of the uncovered spent fuel igniting and, from this, an airborne off-site release of radioactive fission product'.

For Danny, Sizewell had been that old-fashioned thing, a job for life. Back across the green line once more, in the human world, I asked about his retirement plans. Canoeing, his grandsons, a disobedient Dalmatian he and his wife walk on Sizewell beach. 'That's where I struggle a little bit,' he said. 'In my retirement, do I really want a big construction site at Sizewell? If there was a real choice, then no, I wouldn't, but if we don't build Sizewell C, we'll probably never start again, and if we never start again, where do we go, as a country, for power?'

That was the point, as he saw it, the bind: there was no real *choice*. We were speaking during a global energy crisis, with gas shortages in Europe and after a summer of low wind speeds and relatively minimal sunshine hours. Even before Russia's invasion of Ukraine imperilled gas supplies to Europe, EDF, like its counterparts in the 1950s and 1980s, maintained that nuclear was the only way of ensuring national energy security. More than that, nuclear promised an unbroken supply of electricity that did not require the burning of fossil fuels and did not rely, as solar and wind did, on undependable, intermittent phenomena. 'If you look at the overall global crisis, I don't see renewables being the only answer. When the wind doesn't blow and the sun doesn't shine, we have quite a big gap.'

For opponents of Sizewell C, the years and billions it will absorb could more providently be invested in improving domestic energy efficiency and storage technologies for smoothing out the intermittency of wind and solar. It's also the case that nuclear power's very constancy – that it is always 'on', apart from scheduled downtime – means it is an inefficient way of filling the gap. Hinkley Point C, at £23 billion, will by some measures be the most expensive object on Earth. EDF expects Sizewell C to cost £20 billion and take up to twelve years to build, but these figures should be seen in the context of an industry that underestimates both the cost and duration of construction so unfailingly that it can almost be taken for granted that it will run overbudget and overschedule. Since the government decided that China General Nuclear Power Group should not be allowed to maintain its 20 per cent stake, over national security concerns, new partners are being sought. In late 2021, the government introduced legislation for a funding model designed to reduce the perceived risk for potential investors: Regulated Asset Base. RAB guarantees investors intermittent repayments, fixed by a regulator, throughout the course of construction, meaning they can start to recoup their investment before the station has produced either electricity or profit. These payments will be funded not by EDF or the government but by every domestic UK electricity consumer, via a surcharge on bills. For Dieter Helm, Professor of Energy Policy at Oxford University, the funding model only confirms that nuclear power is *inherently* political, 'because it not only involves very capital-intensive and long-lived assets, but also because it comes with environmental-, military- and technology-specific risks on a scale which no private market can handle on its own'.

As well as the cost, and the local disruption and environmental damage, opponents of Sizewell C also claim the site will be vulnerable to flooding and sea-level rise, long after it has been decommissioned. Back in 1992, walking south from Dunwich, W.G. Sebald reported a bleak vision: Sizewell, as he perceives it in *The Rings of Saturn*, does not stand where it is shown on a map, 200 metres inshore, but 'upon an island far out in the pallid waters'. He was given to portents.

Underlying every consideration, financial and logistical and moral, is the question that has always haunted the nuclear industry, and the world: what to do with the spent fuel, which by TASC's reckoning amounts to 650 tonnes at Sizewell B. While EDF won't confirm this figure, it is likely to be an underestimate, as TASC recognises, since the company expects Hinkley Point C (on which Sizewell C will be modelled) to produce a total of 3,600 tonnes over its sixty-year lifetime. Decommissioning of Sizewell A is expected to continue until 2098, while Sizewell B is expected to be decommissioned more quickly, by 2055. But whereas A's spent fuel was sent to Sellafield for reprocessing, B's – and by implication C's – will remain onsite indefinitely.

The government's favoured solution has not changed since 1976: 'deep geological disposal' – burial in a geologically stable repository hundreds of metres underground. In those forty-six years, no British community has agreed that it is in its interests to host such a facility. For now, the spent fuel will continue to accumulate in Sizewell's ponds and casks, attended and soothed like a fairy-tale tyrant's dragon. That is something else the Dome stands for.

'I'm sorry it's complicated for you; it's complicated for us, too.' The speaker was David Brock, a retired planning solicitor and one of the Planning Executive's panel for Sizewell C. The examination phase for EDF's application was nearing its end, and there was an air of frustration among the inspectors. It was evident that time was running out, and the issue of water supply for the planned station was becoming urgent.

The panel had five members: as well as Brock, it included a civil engineer, two town planners, and the lead inspector, Wendy McKay. The six-month examination, which began in April 2021, included fifteen issue-specific hearings, covering questions ranging from traffic and visual impact, to biodiversity and air quality, and, in September: flooding, water and coastal processes.

It was very different from the Sizewell B public inquiry. The Planning Act of 2008, passed by Gordon Brown's Labour government, was nominally designed to speed up the approval process for so-called Nationally Significant Infrastructure Projects such as airports, railways and power stations, to reduce upfront costs for investors. The main component was a series of National Policy Statements (NPS), which set out the government's policies on a variety of infrastructure. Applications for new nuclear power stations were to be assessed 'on the basis that the need for such infrastructure has been demonstrated'; the examining authority was therefore to disregard any representations relating to 'the merits of policy set out in a national policy statement'. This meant that public consultation over new nuclear power stations no longer accommodated discussions about the rights and wrongs of nuclear power itself – its inherent safety, the implications of long-term waste storage, the enduring bonds between the civil and military sectors. It also meant that national campaign groups such as CND and Greenpeace were sidelined. Those, like Joan, who objected to nuclear power in principle could have been forgiven for feeling that the reactors' foundations had already been poured.

The old Sizewell B-style public inquiry, which under Frank Layfield had been virtually unlimited in duration and scope, was replaced by a simplified 'development consent regime', whereby the developer's planning application, once accepted, was succeeded by a public examination lasting no longer than six months. The committee then had three months to make a recommendation to the relevant Secretary of State (Kwasi Kwarteng, in the case of energy infrastructure), who, in turn, would have three months to announce a decision.

On 14 September 2021, nearly thirty years after the Sizewell B inquiry and exactly one month before the end of the Sizewell C examination, the malthouses at Snape were again the stage for a discussion about a proposed nuclear power station six miles away at Sizewell.

As a venue, it cannot have been any more convenient for EDF's representatives than it was for their predecessors in 1983. For local parties, it was more accessible in principle, even if no buses went there. That day's meeting was one of four day-long hearings, which the planning committee had decided to hold in person following an easing of Covid restrictions (these twenty or so hours turned out to be the only in-person element of the six-month examination). The participants sat theatrically lit, like one of those plays based on transcripts of legal hearings, around a rectangle of white-clothed tables, before the dark and silent auditorium. Two unmanned video cameras invigilated. Representatives of the Environment Agency, Suffolk County Council and Northumbrian Water, as well as 'interested parties' like representatives of TASC and Stop Sizewell C, were beamed in over Teams. Sometimes a child could be heard singing in someone's home, or a dog barking.

The government's Climate Change Risk Assessment in 2017 ranked water shortages third in terms of risk to the UK, after flooding and health. Suffolk is described by the Environment Agency as seriously water-stressed, a condition that is due partly to low rainfall and partly to demand from agriculture in a county where irrigation represents 22.5 per cent of water use, compared to less than 1 per cent in the UK as a whole. By 2043, eight years into Sizewell C's anticipated sixty-year operating life, the Environment Agency anticipates a water deficit in the county of around 7.1 million litres per day, based on current supply and demand projections.

The solution agreed between EDF, which would need up to 3.5 million litres of water per day, and Northumbrian Water was that the water company would build a pipeline from the River Waveney, eighteen miles to the north. But then in August, Northumbrian Water received a letter from the Environment Agency, the body that issues water-abstraction licences. The information contained in that letter, Northumbrian Water told the examiners, presented a 'significant risk' that it would be unable to supply '*any* sustainable water' to Sizewell C. (It was unusual to see both underlining and italics in these documents, a combination that, given the circumstances, seemed to carry a mild note of hysteria.)

The Waveney is the river that forms the boundary between the counties of Suffolk and Norfolk. Naturally sluggish, it is prone to flowing very slowly in summer, resulting in low dissolved-oxygen levels. In dry summers thousands of fish have been known to die. Northumbrian Water's intake currently operates all day, every day, and extracts up to 2.8 million litres per day. Following preliminary modelling commissioned by the company itself, the Environment Agency had warned that, in order to preserve downstream water levels, Northumbrian Water's existing abstraction licence was very likely to be reduced by as much as 60 per cent. Further modelling was required to confirm the situation, but if the reduction was imposed, Northumbrian Water would be unable to supply water to Sizewell C not only in the short term but for the foreseeable future, in the absence of alternative sources.

At Snape Maltings, Covid precautions meant there were at most only three or four members of the public present at any one time in the 340-capacity Britten Studio. Sixty-seven of us tuned in from our homes, however, to watch the bench of five examining inspectors facing EDF's council, which was led by Hereward Phillpot QC.

A specialist in planning and environmental law, Phillpot often sought discreetly to transmute the sometimes unfocused or incomplete representations of EDF's experts into a more seductive legalese. He was supported by EDF's planning adviser, John Rhodes, who had been involved in drafting the government's National Planning Policy Framework and previously appeared as an expert witness at the planning inquiry into EDF's Hinkley Point C.

The lead examiner, Wendy McKay, asked Rhodes an apparently simple question: what was EDF's alternative solution if it turned out water couldn't be obtained from the Waveney, as Northumbrian Water now seemed to think was likely? 'What's your plan B?'

'Other options would need to be considered,' he said, but he added that the 'water undertaker', Northumbrian Water, had a *statutory obligation* to provide water, under the 1991 Water Industry Act.

'So,' said Neil Humphrey, one of the other examiners, 'your stance, then, is it's the water company's responsibility to supply you with water, it's not your responsibility to demonstrate you *have* a supply of water.'

'Sir, that's right . . .' said Rhodes.

David Brock, the other examiner, intervened: as none of the panel was, quite evidently, an expert on water law, they would need a written note from EDF, 'succinct, to the point', spelling out the legal position.

Phillpot, hearing the word 'succinct', emphasised the complex nature of the Water Industry Act and that the 'factual position was still evolving'. A note would, perforce, have to set out the full context of the legal position. Would that be acceptable to the examining authority?

Brock leaned forward, pressed the button on his desk mike and folded his arms. 'It sounds to me as though it's probably the best that you can manage.'

On 5 October, nine days before the end of the examination, a further hearing took place – back online, after the fleeting novelty of the concert hall.

While the pipeline from the Waveney was being built – which would take up to four years, if indeed it was approved – a supply of water would be required for construction, up to 3.5 million litres per day. EDF's proposed solution was a temporary desalination plant to turn seawater into fresh water, a solution EDF itself had rejected in January, 'due to concerns with power consumption, sustainability, cost, and wastewater discharge'. Desalination is noisy, expensive and energy-intensive. The plant would remove up to 10 million litres of water from the sea each day, and discharge back into it some 6 million litres per day of saline concentrate and phosphorus. The UK's only current large-scale desalination plant, Thames Water's Beckton facility in London, uses about twice as much energy as a conventional water-treatment plant. Until such time as a permanent electricity supply was installed, Sizewell C's desalination plant would be powered by diesel generators.

But even if a desalination plant were to be approved, the question remained of where water would come from for running the station once it was built.

'There is a likely scenario, at the end of the examination,' said Neil Humphrey, 'that you will have no guaranteed long-term water supply.'

A heavier figure than Phillpot, blank-faced in headphones, Humphrey had a tendency to glance at a supplementary screen positioned above his eye level, giving the impression he was rolling his eyes. He allowed himself a frown. 'Is that a correct statement?'

This time Phillpot was alone in a headset, the skyline of Inner Temple visible through the venetian blinds: 'Well, sir, in terms of where that water would *come* from, there is no guarantee.' He went on, 'We take the view that even if there is not certainty as to what the source will *be*, what that background provides' – the background being the Water Industry Act – 'is a sufficient certainty to ensure that there would *be* a source.'

'So in the applicant's view, you understand that there won't be a guaranteed water supply at the close of examination, but you believe that the water company will provide the water at some point in the future?' Surely, Humphrey went on, 'there must be a scenario where a water company *cannot* identify a sustainable source of water. That is a risk, is it not?'

'They may not be able to identify, *now*, a sustainable source of water,' said Phillpot. Nevertheless, 'It's not a situation where water undertakers can simply say, well, we can't find a source.'

It turned out that while the Water Industry Act does stipulate that domestic premises, including Sizewell C's proposed worker-accommodation campus, have to be supplied, Northumbrian Water is under no absolute duty to supply water for *non*-domestic purposes, if the regulator, Ofwat, deems that doing so will be unreasonably costly or jeopardise existing commitments.

At the end of September, the two firms signed a statement of common ground, agreeing that the water undertaker would 'use its reasonable endeavours' to supply Sizewell C with a non-domestic water supply 'as soon as reasonably practicable', on condition that EDF agreed not to sue Northumbrian Water if it failed to meet its duty to provide a *domestic* supply for the up to 2,400 workers in its accommodation campus.

By the time it became apparent that, save for the sluggish Waveney, no long-term water source had been identified, the end of the examination was nine days away. The final water modelling would not be completed in time, there could be no extension to the examination, and it was too late for cross-examination. Northumbrian Water confirmed that it would be unable to supply Sizewell C with one drop of water during construction. The desalination plant EDF had originally proposed as a temporary measure would therefore have to meet all the site's needs for the up to twelve years the power station would take to build. Beyond that time frame there was no plan.

Like its assurances on the malfunction-prone European pressurised-water reactor, EDF's assurances on the availability of water – 'that there would *be* a source' – were consistent, it seemed, with the entire industry's foundational article of faith: that a solution will be found for sparing the world from the 250,000 tonnes of spent fuel that already exist, including the hundreds of tonnes sitting at Sizewell B, and the thousands more that will be produced by Sizewell C.

That there will *be* a solution, in other words, because it is required that there be a solution.

In late January 2022, about a hundred people were standing at the entrance to the Sizewell B access road, some of whom I recognised from the protest back in September. There were several red-and-yellow STOP SIZEWELL C face masks, and a woman wearing a bright-green foam dinosaur costume was chatting to a Civil Nuclear Constabulary officer cradling a Heckler & Koch assault rifle.

A week before Christmas, the Planning Inspectorate had written to the Secretary of State for Business, Energy and Industrial Strategy, Kwasi Kwarteng, requesting a six-week extension to its reporting deadline, which had originally been mid January. They needed more time to consider the application, they said, due to no fewer than sixteen material changes EDF had made to its application, including last-minute ones such as the desalination plant. There had also been 'unexpected health issues' among the inspectors. The Secretary of State approved the extension, but asked that the inspectorate build 'greater resilience' into its processes, pointing out that large volumes of documentation and material changes were to be expected in such an application. Future timetables, his office said, should be adhered to, 'so that developer confidence in the certainty of timings . . . is not eroded'.

The crowd outside Sizewell B had been waiting for a while, following a tip-off that Kwarteng was to visit the station for a press call. With a month to go before the Planning Inspectorate's delayed recommendation, it had been announced that morning that the government would be granting a £100 million development loan to EDF, 'to maximise investor confidence' in Sizewell C.

I looked for Joan, but it wasn't her scene. A week earlier she'd shown me an album of photos of the house she'd lived in as a child, the house in Darsham with the pond and trees that were destroyed for Sizewell A. Part of me had assumed that her description of the place, when we'd spoken on Sizewell beach back in October, was tinted by nostalgia, but the pond in the pictures was larger and lovelier than I'd imagined, its surface adorned with flowering lilies and dappled with oak-shade.

After waiting for the Secretary of State for forty minutes, I decided to cut my losses and walked the hundred metres to Noel's yard, where I found him filleting the last of a bucketful of bass he'd caught that morning.

Small ones today, so I bought three fillets. He seemed gently amused by the protest. Each to their own. As he wrapped the fish in newspaper, he mentioned that the Secretary of State had arrived hours ago, he was already inside. The protesters had missed him.

That night, Kwarteng appeared on the TV news: the funding package, he explained, represented a 'green light for new nuclear capacity'. Over his shoulder, the Dome looked as two-dimensional as a stage flat, and I understood that it was being made to stand for something else: the future. ∎

Kevin Childs, 1981
Courtesy of the author

BEYOND CONVERSION THERAPY

Kevin Childs

S unday morning was a hard ritual. Breakfast consisted of fried eggs, sausages, bacon and toast, and a big pot of steaming tea. And once it was done and the dishes washed and dried and put away, my mother would pose the question: 'Are you coming to Mass?', knowing full well that the answer was always a negative; and a slight frost descending over her as she put on her coat and gloves, and my father, who was already waiting at the door, suited and booted, the car keys in his hand, frowning just a little, casting a shadow over the sunlight coming through the glass panes.

In my memory at least, it is always the same. I was sixteen. My brother, three years older and away at college, had already lodged his opinion of the Mass a few years earlier. He seemed to get away with it without much protest. My sisters, who were even older, just went with the flow when at home. But I was the youngest. I had been an imagined treasure, all sweetness and light and compliance, until I became, in their eyes, a stroppy teenager. And then there was the other thing.

I no longer believed in God, at least not in any sense or manifestation the Pope would recognise or approve, so what was the purpose of my going to sit in a cold, damp church in the shadow of the Malvern Hills and listening to a priest remind me of what a sinner I was. I already knew it. I knew that God, the God of Abraham and Moses,

God the Father and God the Son didn't love me. I knew that I was not and never would be one of the elect of any denomination, let alone the Catholic Church. I knew because I had been told, week after week, year after year, from the very first inclinations when I was about eight or nine, from the first communions and confirmations and conversations between grown-ups when they thought I wasn't listening or didn't understand.

I was a homosexual, an abomination, a sinner of the very worst sort. I dared not even think it, just in case there was a God and he'd know. Aged sixteen, my Sunday shaking of the head at the question was the only protest I had, silent and small, but a protest, nevertheless. And silence was key. If anyone had ever asked me, I'd have reddened and stammered and denied myself a damn sight more than three times. That's what I did at school when bullies asked me if I was 'queer'. They didn't rate my denials any more than my parents would have.

I was never subjected to those rituals I've heard of where the congregation prays away the gay. I was never raged at by a priest smelling of candles and bay rum, nor sent on a 'correctional' course in the woods somewhere – all versions of so-called 'conversion therapy'. For most people like me, those bizarre rituals remained alien because we never admitted to anyone that we were gay. But what I experienced growing up in a moderately devout Catholic household was a form of conversion therapy nevertheless, a therapy which not only the Church and the priest colluded in, but which society itself approved of in those far-off late-twentieth-century days. A therapy my parents couldn't help but administer. If you're like that, be quiet, it's better no one knows.

I've not been entirely honest so far. I knew that silence equalled survival, a diminished half sort of a life, it's true, but survival. This was 1980. Aids, and all the horror of death and the anger and the need to end silence, was still in the future. But I hadn't exactly ignored what I felt. Hidden away in a cupboard by my bedside was a stash of magazines with stories and articles and pictures of people like me – in those days you sent off a money order, and they came in discreet brown paper envelopes, no questions asked about your age. But only I could see them. They were my secret vice.

Then one day, a few months before my sixteenth birthday, I came home from school and my mother had a flinty, ruthless expression on her face. She'd been cleaning my room and she'd found them, despite all my precautions. I remember feeling the colour drain from my face when she confronted me. I was certainly trembling. My father was working in London at the time and came home at weekends. She couldn't tell him, she said. It would kill him. But he would know what had to be done. I should probably see a psychiatrist, they would certainly have to talk to the parish priest. I might have to be sent away. She wasn't a cruel woman, far from it. She's become a very beautiful person, but her life and her beliefs forty years ago hadn't prepared her for something like this. I told her some implausible lie about why my bedside table had gay magazines in it, and she appeared to believe me, or perhaps she wanted the lie to be the truth because that would be easier than telling anyone that she had a gay son.

My father was a difficult man to live with. He was an army officer and then a physics teacher; a strict disciplinarian at heart and something of a tyrant about the house. I was always afraid of his blazing temper, which is why my mother's threat was not an idle one. He could be savage in his punishments and cruel if you didn't do exactly what he wanted. Between the ages of sixteen and eighteen I rarely did, and we coexisted under a hostile truce. Once I'd gone to university, I tried to avoid going home. I spent my twenties hating him, but this was not the father I came to know and love in his old age. By then he'd mellowed, although we still argued over politics, and I don't think he ever actually approved of who I was. But he'd fallen under the spell of my partner, who knew exactly how to engage him and get him to open up about his past and how he really felt.

When I was growing up in his house, religion was his crutch, a justification for his behaviour. He loved the ritual and the hierarchy; he loved the uncompromisingly old-school Pope John Paul II and loathed liberation theology. It's impossible to pinpoint the moment when the religion of love became a religion of punishment. By the time I came into this world, hundreds of generations had been taught that sex was dirty and that homosexuality was worse than murder. Imagine the damage of having that even in the back of your head. Catholic guilt is so often a joke, but when I was fifteen it nearly killed me. Bullied at school and frightened of who I was at home, I had nowhere to turn other than a rope on a tree or my father's Stanley knife. I thought about it many, many times. I've thought about it since.

That sense of worthlessness never leaves you. I developed ways of coping, a secretiveness, screening myself off from questions, adopting a give-and-take relationship with the truth. I've tried to reinvent myself so many times, running away from that worthless child, but I always return to the boy on a train coming home from school and wishing he were dead.

I did once have a conversation with a priest about my sexuality and he told me the damage I'd suffered was because of the sin. But I know it's because of the construct of sin, which has been used to justify so much cruelty and unkindness; the sour taste of which has remained long after sweetness came into my life. I'm not asking for any special pleading – so many are damaged for so many reasons – but can we end this systematic demonisation by faith groups of people, young and old, on the basis of their sexualities or gender identities? It's inhumane, and so are the processes by which that demonisation is controlled.

A policy document produced by the British government has finally, after a very lengthy 'consultation' period, come to the conclusion that so-called conversion therapy, a catch-all for various practices which aim to 'change' a person's sexuality or gender identity, should be banned for under 18-year-olds. These practices are abusive – how could they be anything other? They cause lasting psychological hurt, self-harm and personality disorders. They lead to suicide. They've been condemned by psychiatric bodies and religious leaders as well as human rights experts. But as Jayne Ozanne, a brave and important critic of the practice, has pointed out, most of this abuse happens to adults who are supposedly consenting to it. The government doesn't intend to do anything about that.

Apart from the fact that you cannot consent to abuse in law, it's worth remembering that the injury done by an almost constant drip-drip of poisonous insinuation in childhood and young adulthood would render any form of supposed consent meaningless, other than as a sort of Stockholm syndrome coping mechanism. I escaped this process by rejecting anything to do with faith. I was sixteen. I was a boy. It fractured my relationship with my parents and left me with a sliver of ice in my heart. Those who retain the faith they were brought up in, or that they later joined, have a far harder time negotiating their sexuality or gender identity under the knout of well-intentioned friends and family.

There's a postscript to my story. My parents' parish priest disappeared one day. Between one Sunday and another a stand-in took the Mass and then the stand-in became permanent. No explanation was given other than that the predecessor was unwell and had been sent on a rest cure. He was never heard from again.

One day not long after, my mother was watching the local news, and recognised her old priest being led off by police from an inner-city parochial house on charges of child abuse. For the very same reason, it transpired, he'd been taken away from our pretty little rural church and sent by the bishop as a punishment to a parish full of vulnerable, impoverished children and young adults. And this was the man to whom I was supposed to turn for spiritual guidance.

After that, my mother never really worried much about my not going to Mass.

Sometimes I envy people their faith, when it seems good and nourishing, a thing of beauty rather than brutality. My partner died suddenly a few months ago, and I understand that it would be a comfort to have faith at such a time. I have felt utterly lost. But the kind of faith I long for rarely chimes with the doctrines of established faith groups, whether churches or mosques or synagogues. It has an ancient splendour to it, connected to the time when the rocks and the trees and the rivers were full of gods. And I know that any God who allows cruelty to be done in their name is no God at all, and certainly no God I want to believe in. ■

PHALONNE PIERRE LOUIS
This photo was taken on the set of *Ti Seri Ayiti*, a video series that addresses insecurity and political instability in Haiti.

JOY AND INSECURITY IN PORT-AU-PRINCE

Jason Allen-Paisant

1

We approach. A grey mountain, its surface like the top of a molar, with its ridges and crevices. Brown-grey undulating earth. High and timeless like all mountains. I wonder about all the people walking there; they're right there, though I can't see them. Their number is large, much larger than I can imagine. Everywhere there are people walking. Real people. I mustn't stop imagining them there on the mountain. They live a life that I can't make up in a detached story, can't know from where I am, so far up, in this plane. They live a life that only *they* know. I can know it, perhaps, if I go in. I'd like to go in, into that picture, into the mountain, to see what can't be seen from the outside.

I'm the only Jamaican here, the only one not going home. We fly over the sea again. The sea becomes brown. We move again over land, real land that a human being can know. I can see corrugated rooftops, a canopy of them, and a road that stretches to infinity, a silver silent line. Brown rusted rooftops interrupted by a large factory that makes some kind of statement within this rusted canopy. Around it, space collapses. The factory evokes a feeling of familiar strangeness, a stickiness, a network of interconnected places.

Western media and writing have defined Haiti as a land of catastrophe. But I am interested in knowing what lies beyond the surface of the known, beyond the narrative of catastrophe. The thing is that I approach this land with love, with respect for what its people have done for us, Black people in the diaspora. And this love produces an openness, an open desire for this landscape.

2

It is 20 November 2018. The organisers of Quatre Chemins, the theatre festival I'm here to attend, forbid me from going out on my own. Even the most mundane trips, to the grocery store or to the restaurant at the bottom of the street, must be organised with my designated driver, Préserve, a local taxi man 'assigned' to me and whom I've befriended. A jovial father of four, Préserve constantly warns me not to be deceived by the apparent calm of the streets; they are not safe at the moment, he says, and tells me off every time I walk to the restaurant on my own. The atmosphere here is more tense than I had imagined. There have been many protests in recent weeks. I see '*Kot Kòb Petwo Karibe a?*' ('Where's the PetroCaribe money?') graffitied on the walls of buildings. The government of Jovenel Moïse is mired in what Haitians are already calling the 'PetroCaribe scandal'.

PetroCaribe is the name of the strategic oil alliance which Venezuela signed with a number of Caribbean states, including Haiti, in 2006. The agreement promised that these nations would need to pay only a fraction for their fuel upfront and could defer the bulk of the payment for up to twenty-five years. An incredible boon. The 2 billion US dollars which have accrued to Haiti as a result of this oil alliance are now unaccounted for, and people are demanding answers. They're not just demanding that heads roll; the demonstrations are a kind of uprising against systemic corruption. Thousands of anti-corruption demonstrators, who call themselves 'PetroChallengers', have taken their anger onto the streets in a collective uproar, and this tidal wave of opposition to Moïse and his allies has been met with violent, deadly crackdowns by the police.

The streets pull at me anyway, and I can't help but go out. Besides, I feel deeply embarrassed to have someone come to walk me from my hotel to the main performance area, a bar, less than two kilometres away, so I sometimes walk alone, in defiance of the organisers' instructions. On walls and street corners, I see graffiti referring to '*Petwo*', meaning, the scandal; though I can't help thinking of the family of warring spirits or *lwa* within the Vodou pantheon who bear the very same name.

3

In Port-au-Prince, I walk looking down. On the pavements, uncovered public sewer pits are common. They impose a different way of walking and produce a kind of terror. I could easily fall in, I think to myself. It doesn't seem to me that others are looking down as they walk, that they are visibly exercising my kind of care. I wonder whether the people who walk these streets experience the terror I do, of falling.

Terror is certainly not my only emotion on these streets. I also experience a sense of identification, of kinship. Kinship with the insecurity that shapes life, with this sense of litheness on one's feet – almost of aerodynamism – of turning hand to make fashion. This litheness that's produced when lack of safety (net) is coupled with a deep-seated determination to defy death. I think of Anansi, the West African trickster deity who often manifests in the form of a spider: in moments of difficulty or crisis, Anansi switches from his human form to his spider incarnation. Some say Anansi crossed the Atlantic in the hold of the slave ship. He is the perfect illustration of what I see here, in the way the people move their bodies. It is an engineering of space that's renewed every day, life lived as a choreography.

Nevertheless, I cannot get rid of this sense of terror, and I am not thinking only of myself. One day, walking along Avenue Christophe, in the direction of the FOKAL, the famous cultural institute in Port-au-Prince, I turn to my friend Miracson Saint-Val, an actor and theatre-maker, and ask whether these 'holes' mean nothing to people here. Are people not affected by them? I can't remember his exact reply; however, it had something to do with the idea of knowing – of a kind of kinetic familiarity with the space, a sense of this being part of the landscape. These pits that range in depth from the relatively shallow to the seemingly bottomless manhole are permanent fixtures on the landscape. But Miracson did not romanticise the issue for all that. He went on to tell me about people who disappear – simply disappear: one day, they do not show up, and are never seen again by their friends and families. He cannot put a number on it, but some people conjecture that the pits, many of which are filled with water, may account for some of these disappearances, when, late at night, a hapless walker falls in, and there is nobody around to aid or rescue.

I speak of kinship but realise that to be terrorised by this reveals my own sense of security – the way the space imposes itself on me underscores the fact that my body is not native to this landscape. All over this space, people embody the choreography of moving *with* the hole, contrary to me. I am analysing.

4

I'm thinking about body praxis as I watch a man board the minibus I'm travelling in. He carries a sewing machine in his hand. He cotches his backside on the narrow ledge behind the driver's seat and with his right hand he supports the sewing machine that's now on the roof of the bus. All this has an aura of the temporary and the evanescent, of the moment within a flow, as in a choreography. The door is, of course, left open, as the bus moves along, sometimes scuttling, sometimes hurtling, in the frenetic heave and hum of the Port-au-Prince traffic. I am not trying to exoticise this. I'm familiar with this minivan. So often, I've travelled on one just like it back home in Jamaica. I'm familiar with the door left open simply because there are so many bodies at the exit that it could never be closed; I'm even familiar with the potentially dangerous hanging of hands outside. But now, I look at this scene with different eyes. This is also a different country, and I have never been struck by this choreography of movement as I am in this moment.

It's all normal – nothing could be more normal in this moment and in this space – the man balances his sewing machine for a few minutes till he reaches his spot and calls to the driver, who lets him off, he pays, and continues on his way. I want to plumb the significance of this choreography to me, how it forces me to read the space in a different way. Some may speak of resilience and how it conditions the operations of the body, the way the body adapts to space and its particular constraints. I can't quite put my finger on it. Without idealising it, I am beginning to feel that this sort of balancing allows people to *see* each other in a way that's more present, more open, than the way people see each other in Leeds, where I live. It may be because the way our bodies occupy space conditions what sort of self we are or think we are: moving in choreography involves a heightened awareness of the presence of other bodies. The way traffic moves in Port-au-Prince seems to provide an illustration of this. It's a flow you enter and exit; things do not stop: no stopping, no hesitating, no doubting; there is no room for that here – there's a rhythm and all the participants are entering that rhythm, sensing each other.

5

I have noticed, sitting in a restaurant in the busy city centre of Leeds, certain things about the street outside: pathways and pedestrian crossings neatly marked out, traffic lights regularly punctuating the thoroughfare. But above all, the smoothness of the streets, the way paths are designated, marked out, the way the city is labelled for the walker. Outside the broad window of the restaurant, the pavement is neatly bordered by railings. In French, the word for railing is *garde-fou*. If safety is already associated with the border in much of our thinking, then this word immediately associates a certain kind of safety with the border between rationality and madness. The railing and the marking make me think of how landscape shapes different ways of being a self, different ways of feeling a self.

6

I've learnt, I think, that one of the secrets of Haitian existence is the joy of creativity and the joy of *being* creative through this *danse de l'araignée* – this joy of what Dénètem Touam Bona calls *'l'indocilité du vivant'*, the indomitableness of the creative instinct.

In this sense, re-storying the landscape seems important, not in that it erases the reality of struggle or insecurity, but in that it reframes how we read the landscape, what we are able to see in it. How much can we see the *vivant*? After my first trip to Haiti, I felt that I had never experienced the *vivant* as much as I had in that moment. It is that moment that produced in me a desire to understand the source of this *vivant*. Imagination is not only born out of insecurity; it is part of the endless process of transforming it.

This trip is making you better, I hear myself say; *it is drawing you into love. It's drawing you into a different way of carrying the body.*

7

Pòtoprens fou. A big-car driver won't stop or slow down even after I've signalled to him, asking him to let me cross. Nobody will slow down here. Nobody takes it easy; the city is never easy. The city is never slow. And yet there is a slowness in the manner of people. People take their time, make you wait; everything starts 'late'. Strange intimacy. A director of a government department tells you to come at a certain time, turns up over an hour late for the appointment. Here, everything is happening at the same time. To be able to hold different things in one's mind is its own aesthetic. Port-au-Prince never rests.

And yet . . . there is a kind of slowness at the centre of things, a kind of radial movement.

I walk along the route de Delmas. I stop in an alley, there's a small tavern. The seller offers me a seat when I buy a beer. He says to me, *bwè byè ou ak kè poze epi ou pral peye apre sa* ('drink your beer in peace and you'll pay later'). No pressure, no clock. People are slow. Their hands are akimbo and their eyes are blue from the sea water that fills them. They have the sea in their eyes, visions, a virtual soar. They wake up from time to time, when a friend passes by, greets them, in the rare moments when a customer comes to buy something.

Someone will say, there isn't a lot of paid work here. And that is true, so true – could I ever deny that? And yet, I know – there's something else behind this slowness.

It's the same at the barber shop. Lots of empty beauty salons, except for women, always two women there, under what pretext? Distracted, not really, waiting for a customer to arrive. Everything slow. Suddenly, they see me, welcome me, send for the barber. Yes, there is a barber, where is he? Yes, there is beer. A can of water – we'll get it. We have everything, we just have to go get it.

8

Different conceptions of time coexist and compete in Haiti. Ritual time exists side by side with capitalist time, money-making time, survival time; there are messy, complex relations between them. Or perhaps there's an order that I haven't yet understood. Perhaps this tension is part of what makes Haiti *Haiti*. Even Vodouists embrace, or live with, multiple conceptions of time. People are hustling, trying to survive, or even get rich. Much like in Leeds where I live, there is no day of rest in Port-au-Prince. On Sunday mornings at 7.30 a.m., like every other day, the hawkers (*vendeurs à la criée*) come out with their bells that play an entrancing tune. What is this country in which people never rest? And yet, that slowness . . .

Black people, we always late . . . I imagine that many people know the stereotype. How many times have I myself repeated this? My body has a conflicted relationship with this statement. For centuries, we've been taught to believe that we're lazy; it's part of the narrative of backwardness written and circulated about us, even while our culture is exploited for its entertainment value, for its vibrancy and energy, even when Blackness is exploited commercially for its rhythms and vitality, we're stereotyped as indolent. But isn't Black 'lateness' part of a gestic imaginary? Isn't it an affirmation of a different time-sense that defies clock time and its infinite movement, its irreversible direction? Though not always inherently so, isn't it *also* a refusal, a contention for *unobligated time* within the long shadow cast by plantation slavery? I read the carrying-on, the making-things-last of Black time as a ceremony of refusal, of affirmation of the body's presence, a gesture (small, large, but always willed) of self-(re)possession. The body is the first measurement of time: to reclaim time is to reclaim the body.

I ask whether slowness isn't also an aesthetic strategy, a determination to preserve an inner vitality in the face of what Achille Mbembe has called 'necropolitics', the politics of the disposability of Black bodies. Slowness is, of course, one part of an intersecting reality, of which the other is daily chaos. Here, people live within a state whose level of corruption has reached absurd proportions; they live with the violence of gangs and police killings. Every day is marked by the hard-flowing adrenaline of fear.

9

In Haiti, therefore, people develop survival skills; as a result, their own gestures become repressive. 'When we see a motorcycle behind us, we are afraid, we walk home very quickly, we lock our door', Guy Régis Jr, the festival director, explains to me over dinner at the famous Hôtel Oloffson. Our conversation is primarily about the festival itself, but he wants to contextualise for me what it means to be able to have a festival like this during this time of chaos.

After the nightly performances of the Festival Quatre Chemins, people hang around, often for a long time, to have a drink, to laugh and have conversations among friends. The performance spaces, various in nature, are spaces of liberation, places in which people can feel again that they're in possession of their movements and gestures. These theatre spaces are not formal buildings of the kind that one finds in Europe. All the formal structures have long fallen into disuse, so plays are performed in bars, in squares, in alleys. The Yanvalou bar is the most famous venue. Occasionally, performances are held at the state-run Centre d'Art and at L'Institut français.

One of Guy's plays is performed in an alley, between compactly arranged houses. The spectators lean against the walls that separate the houses from the street. They sit on these walls, or on roofs, where they can get a good view of the performance. The crowd is so dense that people stand on tiptoes to see above the walls, which, though not too high, offer a modicum of privacy to the residents. I'm standing on someone's front-yard terrace; it's as though we have come into their homes. There are hundreds of spectators in this alley. Residents gradually come outside to watch the play.

Another play, *Chemin de fer*, written by Congolese author Julien Mabiala Bissila and staged and performed by my friend Miracson, takes place at Yanvalou, in the Pacot district of Port-au-Prince, a bar with no theatre set, backdrop or props. There is no machinery, no special lighting (except that the playing area is in darkness before the performance begins). It is an ordinary, everyday place, which the performance must make its own. Directly in the spectators' line of vision is a load-bearing pillar. The walls, too, are awkwardly positioned, separating the space where the audience gathers in a circle from another area of the bar in which the actor does most of his performance. The actor is sometimes masked by these asymmetrical walls. But Yanvalou is also an intimate playing space, a place of everyday enjoyment. It's a place where theatre and city intermingle. The arrangement of forms and objects, including protruding structures and a bar counter, forces a direct interaction between the spectator's space and that of the actor: we are sometimes face-to-face; the actor is, at times, almost surrounded. We see and feel him close by, his body brushes against others; there is a fusion between him and the audience. At certain moments, the audience members feel like actors in the performance. They are there in the work, in the guitar music, when the actor sings, in his gestures, when he shakes hands with the audience in a Vodou ritual greeting. His noises, roars and resonances inhabit their bodies. They are driven to react, somatically solicited, through the energy conveyed through the floor. The play appeals not only to the actor's body, but to everyone's. We support him, we laugh with him, we join in his song.

> *Kote'm foule pye mwen y a rantre*
> *Lwa tèt mwen*
> *Lwa fwa mwen*
> *Lwa Ginen mwen, kote ou ye?*

> Wherever I go, they enter me.
> *Lwa* guide of my life,
> *Lwa* of my faith,
> *Lwa* of my ancestors, where are you?

In *Fictions ordinaires*, which is held at the place Carl Brouard, produced by scenographers and video-makers Jean-Christophe

Lanquetin and Catherine Boskowitz along with a team of Haitian theatre-makers, the performance is based on the idea of a 'dream office' where people can simply come to speak each day: *Biwo Rèv Chak Jou.Vin Pale. Festival Teyat Kat-Chemen* ('Daily Dream Office. Come Talk. Festival Quatre Chemins'). For ten days, they set up this '*biwo rèv*' in the yard of a house on the edge of the square. Their purpose is to explore marginalised places where people meet, make plans, organise their lives, 'despite everything'. The participants ask questions of the people they meet in the street or who come to this yard; *they* too must answer people's questions. These dialogues produce narratives and exchanges, some of them surreal, from which short video, sound and theatrical pieces are made. They're presented later that evening, in the middle of the square.There are two screens, one where the Franco-Haitian team project text written by themselves, and the other on which we see a video of the authors writing and reading in real time.

As the performance begins, the crowd is swarming around the readers, making it difficult to move. The voices of the readers grow indistinct, squashed to a drone hardly discernible from the noise of the crowd.What is interesting to me at this point is the crowd itself, as people jostle each other for a view, as the throng of spectators bares down on the performance space. The children hang on the readers' every word: some are hoisted on the shoulders of parents and watch motionless. In the end, none of the meaning of this presentation (or very little) has to do with the words being said.

10

Je n'aime pas le public sécurisé ('I don't like secure audiences'), says the director Marc Vallès to me. The remarks send me back to my earlier thoughts about security, and the way we walk, move, sit, take the bus, attend the theatre, as an *I*. Lack of security creates so many different

ways of being a body. Among these spectators, I live and feel the
body – even my own body – as *habitable*, as if awaiting others,
awaiting to be jostled, touched, moved. These gestures are owned;
in here, the bodies belong to themselves.

11

Today, I'm being schooled by the houngan, the Vodou priest, Erol Josué:

> When you fall into a trance, possessed by a *lwa*, you lend
> your body to that spirit inside you, which will play its
> role, which will be *itself* in your body, in your head.
> I don't know where I am . . . I feel something coming
> into me; at some point I feel something coming out, and
> I become myself again . . . But there are other dimensions
> in which you remain fully conscious . . . you say, today I
> feel the presence of Ezili, I feel more like a woman today,
> I'm in a cosy atmosphere that's Ezili. Another day I feel like
> Ogou, I am a warrior. I come out of here, my collaborators
> see something, but I'm not playing a role, I'm not scaring
> anyone by behaving like Ogou. It's something that you
> live.
> *Possession* is also a way of life.
> You dream of a spirit that comes to speak to you at
> night, or to caress you at night; you sleep with this woman,
> or with a man who comes to make love to you . . . it's good
> . . . you wake up with that feeling in your mouth. You wake
> up possessed, but aware, with that feeling that will decide
> your day, your relationship with people . . .
> I smell tobacco, alcohol, clairin . . . yet there's none of
> that anywhere around. Is it clairin in my genes, coming to
> me from from the plantation, from the master's house . . .

Is it my *lwa* saying to me, 'I want to drink'? . . . We don't
know, we live with it. We live with it.

12

It's 7 December 2018. I'm leaving Haiti today, my mind filled with
memories of the Vodou ceremony I attended last night not far from
the Bureau national d'ethnologie. I was taken there by Manbo Sisi, my
invitation orchestrated by my friend, Erol. The location was not disclosed
to the general public – which is why I was escorted by the manbo.
We walked from the Bureau nationale d'ethnologie, crossed several
streets amid the dense late-evening traffic – the sun was already setting.

November is the month of the Gede, a family of *lwas* which embodies
the powers of both death and fertility. The celebrations appear to last
into December.

Leaving the *route principale*, we enter a maze of alleys and concrete
houses leading to the *peristil* erected in the backyard of a devotee. The
peristil is a simple, unfussy construction consisting of wooden poles
planted in the ground in a rectangular formation and extending to
a zinc roof. Running along the length of the structure on both sides
are concrete walls – essentially the walls that form the boundaries of
the alley. The *peristil* forms a modest courtyard of about a hundred
square metres. Its floor is the ground – earth: this is essential. In the
interstices between concrete wall and zinc roof, I can see that there
are other houses surrounding us – tucked away at the back of this
alley, the courtyard feels like an interrupted space within a sprawling
bed of tightly packed houses. It's an outside space to the noise of
urban traffic, to the restless hustle of vendors.

I enter the Vodou *peristil* during a pause in the ceremony – no
drumbeats at this point. There are tens of people, men and women,
both young and old, standing to one side of the yard – they look like
spectators; they all look towards the centre of the yard – their boundary

is the line of drummers who sit in a semicircle. The space between that semicircle and the *potomitan*, a decorated wooden pole, seems to be the area of focus; this is the space towards which the attention of the standing spectators is directed: at the moment, the spectators simply talk among themselves, but their bodies are directed towards the space, as if it had a kind of magnetic pull. Some people on the outskirts move around; new entrants greet and are greeted by others.

I've arrived after a moment of trance. A handful of dancers dressed in white look drunken in their gestures. They walk about, exchanging words with other people, but they are restless. Something is about to happen.

I see a young man whose flour-smeared face and torso mark him out as Papa Gede, whose effigy is that of a male revenant, a short, old dark man who wears a high hat and smokes cheap cigars. Papa Gede is hot-blooded and lecherous with a brazen, sometimes crass, sense of humour. It's his bold, overflowing sexuality that links this dancer to him. Flamboyantly and with a teasing manner, he extends his hands and pitches his torso in drunken gestures, tumbles theatrically across the space. The drums have resumed. Playfully, he invites others to join him in the circle.

Those who are 'mounted' by Papa Gede dance to a frenzy, following the young man who has caught the spirit. Some people begin to salute the spirit that has arrived: Papa Gede is here. They exhibit sexual gestures: young men and women greet the manbo, an older woman, by kissing her on the mouth or by moving or brushing against her while dancing in a sexually suggestive way. The manbo gives in to the play of the young men and women.

The manbo orders me to remain seated. I am occupying a place of honour next to her, as her guest. As such, I am often asked for a banknote – or a gift in whatever form – which is to serve as an offering to the spirits. This is play, I can see that. Earlier in his office, Erol had said to me, *The manifestation of the* lwa *is a kind of play, and you have to know how to play.*

Manbo Sisi is obliged to translate for me: *Give me five dollars for the drummer, Give a little something, Give something, anything ... an offering, whatever it is.* To a young man who has just been Gede, who is Gede, I give a £5 note that was in my wallet. Initially, he can't make out where this money originates from, but eventually understands what it is – the manbo helps to explain – and how much it is worth in Haitian gourdes. He's very happy, makes me get up, blows clairin, a spirit made of sugar cane, into my front and back pockets. The manbo explains that this is a blessing, to be prosperous.

At some point in the ceremony, worshippers process with food around the *potomitan*, the central wooden pole by means of which, it's believed, the *lwas* enter the earth and the bodies of the faithful. They offer rice, chicken, sodas and a large cake to the *lwas*. Then, once the food is offered, a large portion of it is distributed, and is eaten. The faithful should not take the food themselves. Those who transported it give it to them.

Erol has arrived. He performs an elaborate greeting with his entire body, a greeting, he explains afterwards, only performed among Vodou initiates. Again, after the feasting, there is movement in the ceremony, beating of drums. To precipitate the trance, the drums are beaten more frenetically. I watch Vodouizan retracting their legs, pitching themselves back and forth, as if intoxicated, falling to the ground. Only one person is fully 'gone' by the end. But after about fifteen or twenty minutes, the spirit is gone.

It struck me that the *Seremoni* has something to do with endurance. People keep going and going; the ceremony goes on for hours. Through successive manifestations (catching the spirit), dancers get closer to trance – this is a rite of endurance. Time is suspended in the ceremony – the time of work, etc. Here, time is orchestrated by the body, not by the clock. This is a mockery of what is not the *Seremoni*, what is not this festivity, and this trance. But it is also a space of care, a place where the community cares for itself, where its members care for each other. For hours, tens, if not hundreds, of people, are entranced in dance and song, in a visceral, visual, embodied poetics.

Here, time and space fuse in our perception to become one substance, and people rendered invisible by society's daily grind can feel that they're still *there*, that they belong to themselves. In this death-defying, joyful dance to defy limitations, time belongs to them; they can take it, they can occupy their moment.

*

Today, we're in a very different time. Jovenel Moïse, the president who had just come to power the year before I visited Haiti in 2018, is now dead, assassinated by mercenaries allegedly hired by some of his local political opponents. The political chaos has created conditions that have favoured the return of gang warfare. Haitians are as if drugged by the catastrophic situation that they hear news of all the time on the radio.

I asked Guy Régis Jr why he persisted in hosting Quatre Chemins, despite the risk and insecurity of organising crowded evening events at a time like this. It turns out that, for many, the safest time to be out in the city is the night. Nightlife offers spaces – concerts, bars, shows – in which one suddenly forgets everything that's going on and lets go. According to Guy, going out to have fun, to take part in culture and make art, is a form of resistance. 'The thing is that, for us, art has its place in this country, despite the chaos,' he adds. 'When I saw the benches fill up for my play, one of the first ones to be performed at the 2021 festival, when I saw the people smiling, I found it extraordinary, because for a moment, people forgot that this was no longer Port-au-Prince as we know it.'

What happens in Quatre Chemins, precisely, in these extreme moments, is that after the shows and performances, when everyone is afraid of being kidnapped, people stay – for a drink, to mingle with the artists – they feel good in those spaces. The bars which Phalonne Pierre Louis has photographed at night are also spaces in which people can feel as if they're in a normal Port-au-Prince. ■

PORT-AU-PRINCE BY NIGHT

Phalonne Pierre Louis

THE
WHITE
REVIEW

'Nothing less than
a cultural revolution'
Deborah Levy

YUSHI LI
The Dream of the Fisherwoman - 2, 2018.

MY MOTHER PHOTOGRAPHS ME IN A BATH OF DEAD SQUID

Lars Horn

My mother always wanted me to look dead. Even when a car slammed my body against concrete, skull ricocheting off the kerbstone. When I woke to paramedics – *blood loss, suspected spinal, head blocks.* When the ambulance doors swung open as we took a roundabout, a paramedic grasping the stretcher, equipment hurtling out the back. As I was rushed into the emergency ward, my mother photographed me strapped to the spinal board, blood matting my hair, drenching my once-white Le Coq windbreaker. 'No, don't wake up, look dead, Lars, look more dead.'

'Open your eyes.'

A mantle blurred into view. I sat up, gasped. The bathwater – littered with dead squid – veered, slapped soft bodies against ceramic. I blinked. 'I can't open my eyes underwater. It stings.'

'But I need you to look dead.'

I untangled a tentacle from the plug chain. The water carried it – slack, filmy – past my torso.

'Lars, darling, the photos won't look right if you don't look dead.'

'I'm cold.'

'I can't add hot water. It'll affect the squid. Look, get under there, hold your breath, open your eyes. Come on, I haven't much film.

And I can't waste this, I spent good money at that fishmonger's.'

A fine art teacher, my mother led a yearly trip to Aberystwyth, Wales. During one of these trips, in the communal bathroom of a seafront B&B that hadn't seen an update since the fifties, my mother began a photography project that would span decades of my life. I have modelled in baths, glass cases, on beds, beaches, in forests. My body covered in dead fish, offal, dried flowers, ashes. My body cast, photographed, filmed, watched by gallery audience. My mother's instructions always: *Look dead, Lars, look more dead.*

I peered over the rim of the jaundiced tub at the rotten cork linoleum. My mother adjusted her weight, checked the light balance on her Nikon. A rancid odour lapped up from the dead squid. I could barely detect the cloying mix of bleach and antiseptic that announced the bathroom's cracked mirror and lacklustre tiling. I looked down at my legs, at the squid drifting against my shins. *Look dead, Lars, look more dead.* I inhaled, slipped below the water. Cold swallowed, blunted. I heard the muffled click of my mother photographing me, the squid. I waited one last moment, opened my eyes.

In the emergency ward, the nurse came in and saw my mother taking photos, telling me to open my eyes, close them again, look vacant, look dead. Dead, dead, dead.

'Do you want this woman escorted out?'

I lay on a stretcher in head blocks. The ceiling pulsed: 'No, just the phone, get her to put the phone away.'

'Madam – the phone.'

'But I'm her mother.'

Always that: *I'm her mother.* In supermarket aisles, in the car, on the street: *I shat you out my body like a melon, I can do what the fuck I want.* And even when a doctor poked at the glass and grit in my face, pushing so roughly that I breathed sharp. When another doctor saw this and lost his shit, medics rushing to pull the first 'doctor' away from my body. When the actual physician explained that a psych patient sometimes stole a white coat and walked A&E pretending to be staff, even then, how I groaned, began to laugh, how my mother and I laughed. *Look more dead, Lars. Dead. Just look dead.*

For her funeral, my mother wants a black carriage drawn by black horses to carry her coffin down the high street. She wants a jazz band to follow in her wake, play 'When the Saints Go Marching In' under the banner: MUSIC TO DIE FOR.

When I queried the cost and feasibility of the Victorian ceremony, my mother replied, 'It is my dying wish.' (She is not dying.) 'You must do it or live with the guilt, because I won't be forgiving anyone. I'll be dead.'

My mother recently said that she will have to record herself performing her own service, because no one else will do it with sufficient passion.

On this point, I am inclined to agree.

For the remainder of our time in Aberystwyth, no one used the bathroom my mother co-opted for the photo shoot. The stench of dead squid had anyone gagging barely two minutes into brushing their teeth. For the entire week, three floors of guests filed round the stairwell, waiting for a ten-minute spot in the establishment's only other bathroom. Waiting there, towel flopped over her forearm, my mother decided to move the project outside of the B&B. The next three days, she photographed me in rock pools, lying face down on the sand. In one negative, molluscs line my back. In another, a severed salmon head rests beside my own.

In Sophie Calle's *Voir la mer* / *See the Sea*, 2011, inhabitants of Istanbul who have never beheld an ocean are driven to the shores of the Black Sea. Calle films them from behind as they unmask their eyes to take in the shoreline. When they are ready, they turn around to face the camera: eyes charged with the sight of wild water. Bodies seen and seeing. Tangled dynamic of artistic means and subject.

My mother drank hard, laughed hard, spoke hard. She spent money she didn't have, said things she didn't mean. She didn't cook, swore by TV dinners, and most certainly did not think everything I did was wonderful. She preferred the phrase 'What are you tit-arsing around at?' to 'How was your day, darling?' When I brought home school projects or 'bits of twonky shite' as she referred to them, she did not pretend they deserved a place on any living-room shelf, but simply took them off my hands, exclaiming, 'God, what am I meant to do with this gobshite?' Quickly followed by: 'I mean, darling, it's *lovely*,' all uttered in the single movement of project to pedal bin.

My mother never wanted a home-made gift or a hand-drawn card: 'Don't be cheap, have the decency to buy me something that's not an eyesore.'

She is not a conventionally 'good' mother. But then, put like that, it sounds like a slow death sentence anyhow.

England, midwinter 2005. An unheated art studio. Modelling for a recumbent full-body plaster cast.

In the abandoned toilet block, snow obscured the awning window. My breath misted the mirror. A pipe dripped. The tube light – its plastic casement pitted with dead moths – flickered. The weather could not have been worse for a plaster cast. I snapped a swim cap over my hair and ears. I undressed. My feet settled upon cold, gritty tiling. Days before Christmas, the building stood empty, cavernous. I retrieved a tub of Vaseline from my bag and applied a layer to my face, arms, underarms, stomach and groin. I smeared the Vaseline over my eyebrows and eyelashes, held on to the sink, blinked.

Prior to a plaster cast, bodily hair must be greased with petroleum jelly. The difficulty lies in never applying so much as to obscure the patterning of the skin – pores, scars, individual hairs – as this gives a high-quality finish and realism to the cast. But too little and the removal of the cast could turn into a slow, full-body wax.

The technician knocked on the toilet-block door, 'You ready?'

'Just the cling film to go.'

'I'll wait, let me know if you need help.'

As a child, I always wore legging shorts for modesty when being cast. But as the fabric absorbs the liquid plaster, the shorts bind to the cast, meaning one has to be cut out of them. Unlike cotton underwear or shorts, cling film repels liquid plaster, preventing the removal of pubic hair or the irritation of sensitive skin.

Pulling a roll of Glad Wrap from my bag, I stretched it over my genitals and taped it in place. I opened the door. 'Ready to party.'

Between the ages of four and nineteen, I modelled for:

> Thirteen full-body casts: ten plaster, two Sellotape, one tissue.
> Three performance pieces: bed, wake, autopsy table.
> Four short films: one in which I sleep with eight others on a wall of scaffolding; a second that shows me surfacing from a bath of black water, gasping on repeat; another whereby I walk in wax shoes until they shatter underfoot; and another still in which I wear paper clothing as buckets of water are dumped over me.

Across those fifteen years, my mother collected:

> Eight animal skulls: lion, alligator, water buffalo, bison, horse, camel, cat, monkey.
> One framed set of Victorian wax dental casts.
> Three life-size anatomical models.
> A turn-of-the-century glass eye (blue).
> Two articulated skeletons: pigeon, frog.
> A taxidermy seagull.
> A child's shoe retrieved from a bog, the mud having preserved its leather and laces since the Middle Ages.

The time we visited Florida, my mother purchased a second suitcase so as to accommodate the shells, coral, shark jaws, snakeskin wallets and sea sponges she'd bought. The 1940s rowing oars required a more elaborate persuasion of air staff.

Customs was never a quick affair.

If my mother found a dead animal, she would place the corpse in a carrier bag and head home to bury it in the backyard.

Six months later, flesh and fur and feathers decomposed in earth, she'd dig up the skeleton.

We did this while drinking lemonade, Diet Coke.

My aunt once helped my mother with a photography project. My mother wrapped her in layers of cling film in the heartland of British suburbia that is my grandmother's back garden. It was midsummer. Each day clung stickily to the next. My aunt, sweltering, fainted. My mother tore her from the plastic as my grandmother marched out of the kitchen: 'What on earth will the neighbours think?' As her forty-year-old younger daughter staggered naked between plastic lawn chairs, a group of dog walkers looked on from the meadow beyond the garden wall. At this, my grandmother reached her limit: 'Even the Labradors are staring.'

Another year, my mother dried flowers by laying them over the living-room floorboards, until we had to jump from one vacant foothold to another. The postman caught sight of me, once, performing this intricate ballet from sofa to kitchen kettle, and I shrugged, not seeing what was so strange about any of it.

A fan heater wheezed across the studio's herringbone floor.

'This is all we've got.' My mother turned from a boiling kettle. 'The other heater's packed up. You still okay to do this?'

'I'll manage.'

Black sugar paper covered the casting studio's windows. Bulbs hummed overhead, shivered light onto a laminated table. On the table, two basins stood beside pre-cut piles of plaster bandage. My mother filled the basins with boiling water, adding a glass of cold to make it workable.

'Right, last calls: lavatory, Vaseline? Anything else you need?'

'No, I'm good.'

Full-body casts run at high cost – studio space, technicians, models, materials. They also require considerable time and logistical coordination. Needing to urinate or defecate during the casting process will cost an artist hundreds of dollars and hours of their time. The cast will have to be abandoned – unfinished, unusable. The night and morning before a cast, I eat plain rice or pasta and drink as little as possible. I also, prior to applying Vaseline or cling film, pass a hot washcloth over my face, neck and chest. The body will soon be cold and covered in warm, wet bandage. The washcloth pre-emptively triggers any need to urinate induced by temperature difference.

I lifted myself onto the table, lay on my side. My mother and the technician adjusted my limbs.

'Bring the arms into the chest, that's it. Now, this arm, lay that atop the other, but not perfectly. Yes, off-centre. And the fingers – don't separate them; they'll be too fragile once cast. Maybe bring the knees up. Can you work on that space across the stomach, between the thighs and the arms?'

The technician clicked on a paint-smattered radio. Static hazed, settled over my collarbone, my ribcage. My mother wetted a strip of two-by-two-inch plaster bandage, pulled it between forefingers to remove excess moisture, and smoothed it onto my skin. Rubbing the wet bandage, she distributed the plaster of Paris across the webbing. The technician repeated the process along my feet. Christmas hits whined from the radio. The smell of plaster eddied off my body – mild, powdery. I closed my eyes, exhaled.

A full-body cast, performed by two people using plaster bandage, takes around three hours – work speed and ambient temperature depending. That midwinter day, with temperatures groaning below zero, with a team of only my mother and one technician, the cast would take four and a half hours. Curled on my side, the majority of my weight fell on my hip and shoulder. After only fifteen minutes, my body ached. The cast would prove one of the most demanding I would ever endure.

After my parents separated, I lived alone with my mother from the age of four until I left home at eighteen. We rarely ate together, instead using the dining table to assemble photographs, severed talons, wings. In the evenings, we read or worked in separate rooms. The bathroom was different.

My mother says that the best thing I ever did for the house was to put a chair in the bathroom. While this might suggest just how little I did for the home – a sentiment my mother would back – I'd like to think it also points to how we used that room. To the late-night talk, words clouding vaporous in steaming heat. How, at hours of disjoint from work and routine, we were able to relinquish something more honest of ourselves, one of us bathing, the other sat listening as thoughts fell into water. How it has always been in a bathroom that my mother and I find an understanding. How water – crashing, stilling, water carrying a body exhausted – how it engenders a rare generosity.

My grandmother tells stories of my mother as a teenager deciding to dress 'as an artist', which is to say, sporting two flannelette dressing gowns beneath a cape to the grocer's, or a fur coat held together by some thirty safety pins to church. Regardless, my grandmother made her elder daughter walk several paces behind her.

When, at two years old, I learned the word *no* and screamed it every time someone tried to put me in a dress, a girl's bathing costume, a girl's T-shirt, shorts, underwear, anything pink or pretty, my mother only stood back and said, 'This kid's as queer as they come.' She watched as I picked out boys' toys – cork guns, plastic swords, Action Men, Mighty Max, a boy's twenty-one-gear bike. Watched as I chose boxer shorts, green nylon swim trunks, as the hairdresser handed me a magazine and I turned and turned the pages until there was a picture of a man advertising perfume, until I pointed to his crew cut, looking warily upwards to see if it would be approved.

The bathroom back home is smallish and hasn't seen a renovation in decades. The doorknob crashes off the door. The tub lies scrubbed of enamel. A bullet hole fractures the window from the night when a neighbour shot an air rifle at the lit pane, my mother's silhouetted body stepping out of range by seconds. Paint peels from the floorboards. There's no shower, only a rubber mixer head that hangs, limp, from the bath taps. A bathroom accessory so 1950s in style that my mother is perpetually worried Boots will stop carrying it. The tiling – a 1970s beige-brown stripe – frames all this across two walls, wavers beneath the single, hesitant bulb. It is the one room we've never had the money to redecorate.

When I think of my mother, it is almost always of her in this room with its copper boiler that takes two hours to heat, in this room holding out against all odds, her shoulders rounded in the tub, water rippling over her limbs.

In the time we've spent in the bathroom, mirrors fogged with steam, a sliver of light spilling round the doorframe from the landing, my mother has told me she's tired, no, really tired, my love; she's voiced her fears, consistently asked for and ignored my advice; she's recounted who's engaged or pregnant or getting divorced at work; she's told me we're in debt, that the house needs remortgaging a third time; that she wants to do an installation piece of nine sleeping women and will I participate? She has asked what the fuck I'm playing around at, told me I'm making a mistake. Usually, I come back and tell her she was right, maybe it takes a night or several years, but she's almost always right. It's a strange thing to acknowledge: that your mother knows you better than you know yourself.

I do not remember the physiological changes of puberty, do not recall developing breasts or hips. They all remain things that my body renders thankfully impossible to excavate. But I do remember my mother telling me that I'd find a way, in this skin, find a way to articulate the body as tension, as contradiction. How, with time, these edges might even cohere – brief flickering of moth to light.

My mother, a woman who in childhood photographs looks like a boy. A woman who, at university after another student was murdered in her building, shaved her head and wore men's clothing. A woman who frequently passed as male. A woman who once said to me, 'If times had been different, I'd have turned out like you.'

I came out as queer while my mother drew a bath.

'Fucking *finally*.'

She spun the faucet fully open, water collapsing upon water.

'Thank God we don't have to play along with that any more.'

The technician dried her hands on a chequered rag. She took a pair of scissors, cut a plastic straw into short lengths. Modroc covered my entire body except my face. The radio wavered – dull, indistinct, distant. My body shivered. Pain seared across my hips, ribs, shoulders. I controlled the urge to shudder.

'Almost there, my love.'

My mother emptied, refilled the basins.

The technician crouched to my eye level: 'We're going to cover the forehead, eyes and jaw now. I'll let you know when we're starting the mouth. After that, it'll be one sound for *yes*, two for *no*. All right?'

Steam rose off the basins, warped the light.

'Okay, Lars, close your eyes.'

As plaster bandage layered across my eyelids, the reddish glow of backlit blood extinguished. Darkness swelled.

I heard the technician's voice near my ear. 'Mouth now.'

I closed my lips, made a noise in my throat. The technician slowly inserted a section of plastic straw in each nostril.

'Can you breathe?'

Noise in my throat.

The radio slurred into the darkness. Plaster stung my eyes, itched my mouth. Air rattled – thin, weak – through the straws. The metal legs of a stool dragged across the floor. A kettle boiled. Spoons clinked against mugs.

'An hour's drying time to go, Lars.'

There is a moment during a full-body plaster cast, after several layers of Modroc have been applied, after the eye sockets and mouth have been sealed into darkness, when only two nostril holes or a straw between the lips feed your breathing, a moment when you panic – even after thirteen casts and accustomed to the process.

I counted, slowed my breathing.

When I was fourteen, an autopsy table retailed at £1,000. My mother sold off antiques and flipped through pages of beds, stretchers and stainless-steel tables in a medical supplies catalogue. One week later, an 'Autopsy Table ST 10/500 Moveable' was ours.

For three separate performance pieces, I lay on the table, my body partially covered by a white sheet. Some twelve hours in total. My mother announced the project as a doctor might recommend a cure: 'Half a day's death to temper your youth, it'll do you a power of good.' I flexed my face muscles – the plaster tugged at my eyelashes. I flexed again. My eyelids peeled from the cast. Eyelashes tore from their ducts. I rolled my lips, tasted blood as plaster rent skin. I breathed within heavy carapace. The cast compressed my ribcage, my back, my throat, my cheeks.

'Lars, we're almost there. The plaster needs another twenty minutes. Can you hold on?'

My body struggled to convulse, to vomit. I breathed through the straws – slow, insipid. My eyes watered. My nose ran. My body shivered.

'Lars?'

A cast cures by leaching the model's body heat. It rigidifies, shrinks. The cast increasingly restricts the chest cavity, forcing a slow, shallow kind of breathing. Yet, amid this, one must maintain a state of absolute immobility, of perfect stasis. *Look dead, Lars, look more dead.*

Aged four and modelling for my first full-body cast, I screamed when the technicians plastered over my eyes and mouth, screamed so fiercely that the technicians had to rip the plaster from my face and remove the rest of the cast early.

Thinking I was going to suffocate, I shouted for the technicians to 'get the fucking bastard thing off me'. The technicians all agreed: 'Definitely your kid, Sheri.'

Another time, during my twenties, my mother asked last minute if I could come to her exhibition opening earlier than arranged. I apologised: I worked, otherwise I would have. The next day, I arrived at the gallery. Pushing through the doors, I found my mother lying naked in a vitrine of offal and maggots. The maggots seethed through her hair, crawled over her face, between toes, fingers, over her stomach.

She calls it a scheduling error. I call it divinely ordained escape.

The irony is, had she simply explained that she needed a model for maggots and entrails, I'd have called in sick to work. I doubt it's even a lie when one spends the day beneath heaped, rotting death.

Years later, when my mother learned that the woman I would eventually marry was not only a writer – a career of which she approved – but also Puerto Rican, she couldn't have been happier: 'Puerto Rico has the most exceptional funerals; the extreme embalming there is an art. You know, Lars, I thought about having you done that way, if ever you died first.'

Only in death would my mother ever have me model as alive.

One tends to imagine bodily sensation increasing as the modelling process progresses: how levels of physical discomfort rise due to cramps and muscle fatigue, how extremes of temperature seem to escalate. And yet, even if I experienced this early on, even though I still contend with discomfort during casts, performances and film-photography shoots, so often, modelling is a way through, even past discomfort. Odours dissipate. The fetid loses its aversion. Maggots, flies, butchered meat – all cease to cause repulsion. The body can accommodate. Become a thing of changing dimensions. Of breadth. Space in which the world can rearticulate.

In Rachel Whiteread's *Untitled (One Hundred Spaces)*, 1995, the vacuous undersides of one hundred chairs are rendered solid, cast in bright, gummy-like resin. The sculptural forms – cuboid, the occasional concave scroll of a former spindle – stand in regimented lines. I remember a description saying they were all taken from the undersides of bathroom stools. Now that I look again, years later, I can only find it listed as chairs. I wonder if that was ever true or if I only imagined them as bathroom stools, subconsciously saw those strangely aqueous objects as echoes. The river of one's own life sweeping outwards, swallowing anything within reach.

Even in my teens, when my mother drank heavily, when I would draw the bath for her near midnight, help wash her back as I placed pint after pint of water on the rim for her to drink, even when I made sure she dried off, put on pyjamas, got safely to bed, we still talked. Even if she was drunk, she told me how and why she wasn't coping, the job, money, raising me, how everything was veering, not working out right.

It was also in that bathtub, years later, that my mother returned the favour after I had a breakdown, after I stopped talking, my back a wreck of torn muscle tissue, my body swollen, lethargic. Decades since she'd last helped me wash, she soaped my skin, told me this would pass, not to worry, that of course I'd think and read and write again, that I'd not always be dependent. Only years later did she admit that she feared I'd never get back to myself.

She washed my hair, my face. My mother, not known for her sentimentality. Once, a friend phoned, said, 'Sheri, my husband's been having an affair, I think we're getting a divorce.' My mother replied, 'Okay, my baked potato's just cooked, so I'll eat that and phone you afterwards.' My mother, who will eat her dinner before listening to your heartache. This woman carried me that year, knelt at the bathtub to wash me, sat next to me as I hyperventilated on the bedroom, the living room, on any and every available floor.

My mother gives her best advice in the bathroom. She'll tell me when I've fucked up, when a situation is or isn't my fault. She'll tell me how the book she's reading really does put my situation in perspective, and it's often true because medieval plague and superviruses and the minds of serial killers do have a knack of doing that. She tells me when to get my shit together. Most of all, though, not to be too hard on myself when it all goes arse over tit, because it will, because it has to if you are to live.

When I tell people about growing up with my mother their responses usually fall somewhere between disbelief, humour and concern. As for how I felt: I remember arriving at university, this supposedly wild and exciting time of one's life, and realising a few weeks in that never had my life been so ordinary, never had I been so perfectly, painfully bored.

Barring performance art, society tends to understand artwork as the static end product of a creative process. As terminal object, relic. As artefact. Objects to which we come in temporal reverse. I am most interested in artwork as creative process. In the dynamics that occur before, and up to, any final outcome. I like the slipperiness of that. Revising, refining, hauling to surface. The physical effort, bodily gesture. I want the slow plasticity of binding action into object. Collisions of body and media. Physicality collapsing into physicality.

There is something about bathrooms that approaches modelling. The stasis. Being in one's skin, differently. A room of water. Of piped current. The particular kind of intimacy – with oneself, others. How water carries a body. Takes time, memory, takes physicality within the tide of itself.

After some four hours, my mother slid a hand between the cast and my skin. She pushed into my back, my thighs, drew a thumb along my calf. I made small movements, lost hair, bled. I emerged cramped, shaking, bruised. The technician supported my weight as I staggered, legs folding, to the toilet washbasin. The technician held me as my body juddered, applied a warm washcloth to the bruising that stretched from my thigh to my ribs. For the next hour, I collapsed.

The bodily depletion after an extensive cast defies easy category. The lack of coordination. The inability to immediately regain autonomy.

Muscle seizure. Blood seething up the arms and legs. This strange reacquaintance with movement, temperature, with sound. A shaking of death from limb. The instability of something newly birthed.

Photographs make me uncomfortable. The frontal smiling. To fashion oneself, pose. But to have one's body curated, articulated and placed. To have it arranged in unfamiliar ways. I like that. How it forces me to feel my body differently. Its strange pace. To hold the body in stasis, duration leadening the limbs with new weight. To feel the shifting texture as one occupies space. I like the estrangement of modelling. And its strangeness.

Being transmasculine, my body largely resists feelings of ownership. The sensation of waking within limbs that one recognises, of finding oneself reflected, to sense propriety over one's body – I have never felt that. I am still surprised, even after thirty years of living in this skin, when I catch sight of myself in mirrors. It still manages to come as a slap of cold water in the early-morning light. I experience my body as vessel, as carrier, as God-given, perhaps. Bearer of a disjointed entity – watery thing that doesn't fit the body I walk within. Maybe that is why modelling sits comfortably with me: my body rarely feels like my own, anyhow. I am grateful for my body, for how it moves me through the world, but I do experience it as distance, as transient shell that I will walk out of in the same way I walked in. I identify with the gazes put upon it. Their exteriority. To look *at* myself more than *as* myself. To experience oneself from within, but, also, crucially, from without. ∎

DONAL STURT
Half a Diptych with Added Lipstick, 2017

BLUE-EYED MUGGERS

Alejandro Zambra

TRANSLATED FROM THE SPANISH
BY MEGAN MCDOWELL

1

Once, I defended my father. Physically. It was a summer morning, and a mugger was about to kick him while he was down.

'That was in 1990, right?'

'Are you writing about me again? Enough is enough!' says my father.

For some months now, my father has been calling my son every Saturday and Sunday morning. Now that my son is almost four years old, my father has, unexpectedly, become an attentive long-distance grandfather: him in Chile, us in Mexico, separated by too many kilometers and almost two years of pandemic.

My son waits for those calls. He wakes up as always between six and six-thirty, and he comes running into my room, which is his, because at some point during the night he woke up and called to me and climbed into our bed, which to him is his mother's and his, and I went to his bed, which is also, as such, a little bit mine.

'Dad, has Grandpa called yet?' he asks me eagerly.

I yawn and pick up my phone, and when I check my messages there is always one from my father that says 'I'm ready'. My dad gets up early, he's gotten up early his whole life. I belong to the category of fathers who would always like to sleep in just one more hour. My dad belongs and has always belonged to the category of early-bird fathers. And on top of that, because of the time difference, in Chile he's in the future: three hours in the future. Maybe it's a good thing for fathers to live three hours in the future.

I open the curtains to let the daylight in, but the sun hasn't risen yet. My son piles up his books and clambers up to reach the light switch while he chats enthusiastically with his grandfather. They venture plans, immediate and urgent ones; it's going to be a long and intense call, it always is, they'll talk for at least an hour.

During the week he gets dressed almost by himself, or we help him but favor the fiction that he dresses himself. On weekends, however, I dress him quickly, we go straight down to the living room and lean the phone against the wall, angling for a wide shot, like a security camera's. I make coffee and try to get breakfast going while they talk, but sometimes the phone falls over or my son moves out of frame.

'Alejandro, please, I can't see the boy,' my father complains instantly, like a diner who found a hair in his soup.

His tone harbors the same authority as always, but there's a friendly shading: I suppose he knows I'm busy slicing a papaya or keeping an eye on the quesadillas. I go over to restore the communication, proceeding with efficient know-how, a little like a roadie mid-concert. Sometimes I take advantage of that break to say something, to tell him a little something.

'I'm not writing about you, Dad,' I lie.

'Why don't you write about the kid instead? He's a lot more entertaining than me,' he says, and it's very true.

'Well, I was thinking about that time we were assaulted. That was 1990, right?'

'Right.'

I don't use the informal 'tú' with my father, I never have. My sister does. For many years I didn't notice that difference. But there's an explanation.

In my father's family everyone uses 'tú' with each other, and my sister inherited that habit. I was closer to my mother's side, and maybe that's why I inherited her custom of using the formal 'usted'. Sometimes, using the formal tense with my father or mother seems warmer to me. But it's not. It's colder, it marks a distance. A distance that exists.

'You're going to write about that assault? A whole novel?'
     'No, I couldn't get a whole novel out of that.'
     'Make it a whole novel, embellish it a little. Is it my biography?'
     'No.'
     'I'm going to write your biography too, just you wait. I'll tell the whole truth then.'
     'And what are you going to call that book?'
     '*Ways of Losing a Son.*'

2

The story from 1990 is simple, perhaps its only peculiarity is that I've never been able to tell it. That is, I've told it a thousand times, but only to friends, in the midst of those long gatherings when everyone riotously offers up their old anecdotes – the kind of party I miss so much now, in the pandemic. It's an after-dinner story, to be told in the characteristic cheerful, good-humored tone in which such tales are told.

     I was fifteen, and my father was . . .

     I get out the calculator, let's see: my father was born in 1948, so that morning in 1990 he must have been . . . 1990 - 1948 = 42 years old. Forty-one, because it was February, and he was born in August.

     My father, at forty-one, would have considered it humiliating to need a calculator for such a simple operation. Even today, at seventy-three, my father would come up with the answer without hesitation, in less than a second. He wouldn't give the impression of having solved a math problem at all.

Back then, when I was fifteen – no, fourteen, because it was in February and I was born in September.

Back then, at fourteen years old, that summer of 1990, I would have done the math in my head, too.

'My dad was on the ground and he was shouting for them to please let him look for his contact lens, and the blue-eyed mugger was going to kick him while he was down, but I managed to kick him in the balls.'

That's the story, in essence. I want to tell it slowly, like someone reviewing a polemical play frame by frame. Like someone figuring out whether the ball hit the defender's hand or not. Like someone looking for a continuity mistake.

The times I tried to write this story before, I did it in the third person. I almost always try in first and third person. Sometimes also in second, like my favorite novel, *A Man Asleep*, by Georges Perec. In the end I choose the voice that sounds most natural, which is never the second person.

There's something about this particular story, though, that made me try it only in third. Maybe because lately I have reconciled with the third person. Because everything that happens, happens for everyone. Unequally, but it happens. For everyone. And in spite of the asymmetries, in spite of those differences, I feel like everything that happens to me happens in the third person.

3

During those calls my father and I speak little, sometimes not at all. They are the ones who talk, my father and my son. If I interject, my son will eagerly include me in the game, but if he gets the sense that my intention is, so to speak, informative – if I want to check in, for example, regarding my father's feelings about the pandemic – he gets mad, sometimes very mad.

My father and my son plan trips to Mars or to Chile, which for now seem equally improbable. They mix Spanish with an invented language that sounds like a kind of Russian with a German accent. Other times the game consists of improvising something that they call 'a meeting'. Their conversations are fast, confused, funny, delirious. At times my father's deep and hurried Chilean loses ground to my son's pristine Mexican. But they understand each other, always. My son gathers a bunch of stuffed animals and my father does too, because over these years he has mitigated the distance by buying stuffed animals to give my son once they can finally see each other. My father becomes the supervisor of that small crowd of stuffed bears that look like dogs and dogs that look like bears. My son behaves rather like the charismatic leader of a squadron of space vagabonds.

'You want to say hi to your grandma?'

'Yeah.'

This only happens sometimes. Only sometimes does my mother participate in these calls. And for a few minutes, no more. My mother says tender words to my son at the wrong time. He listens to her with wavering curiosity. Hearing my mother's voice, seeing her face out of the corner of my eye, moves me, though she spends only a moment in the limelight, her role is just a cameo, because she doesn't want to play and the call consists of playing. She'll get mad – pretend-mad, I assume – when she hears my son and my father inventing the dishes served up at Restaurant Gross: vomit puree, poop soup, pee lemonade, snot casserole, among many other options that my son celebrates passionately.

'Horacio, please, stop it,' my mother tells my father.

Sometimes my son turns his back on the call. He starts to draw, for example, while his grandfather talks. He doesn't leave the game, drawing is part of the game, and maybe ignoring his grandfather is too. Even as my father grows tired of insisting, my son knows that the call hasn't ended. I like that absurd and beautiful form of company, that silence filled with activity. During recent weeks, since I started writing this text, those are the moments I've used to ask my father about the details of this story, or even read him a few parts of it. He listens to me with a mixture of impatience and genuine interest.

4

When I was fourteen, my father was still taller than me. I understand we reach our definitive height at around twenty years old. In any case, I was a skinny, hunched-over, delicate kid who certainly didn't look capable of defending a father who was stocky, brawny, athletic, with enormous hands. A goalie's hands.

My father's were and are the hands of *someone who has worked with his hands*. Real work, like loading crates of vegetables at the Renca market. At nine, ten, twelve years old, my father sold fruits and vegetables at the market in Renca. My father's hands also served to block goals and interrupt penalties. My father's entire body has been, in general, useful. And it would have been much more so if not for his weak eyes.

He wanted to do military service, he wanted to become a policeman, he almost became the third goalie in the Colo-Colo youth divisions, but none of that worked out, partly because of his sick eyes. In all the photos of him as a young man, he's wearing some Coke-bottle glasses that give his face the appearance of a mask. I inherited a manageable myopia, reasonable and even operable, though I never seriously considered it (the very idea of lasers on my eyes is terrifying). At fourteen I'd already been prescribed glasses, but I never wore them; I still hadn't reached the age where leaving the house without glasses would be suicide. An age I reached a while ago now. Even so, with my myopia and astigmatism and my recent nearsightedness, my eyesight is still better than my father's at forty-two and my father's at seventy-three years old.

When it's said that someone works with their hands, no one thinks about writers. Rightly so. We have the hands of mediocre pianists.

My father is not a writer, he never has been, never wanted to be. He was never interested in poetry. Although I do remember a day when he wrote a poem.

'It can't be that hard, Chile is a nation of poets,' he said.

I don't remember the chain of events or words that led to that phrase. But suddenly my father grabbed a napkin and the pen he only used for signing checks, and without hesitation he wrote a poem that he read aloud to us immediately. We applauded. We were his captive audience. A generous audience. Too generous, indulgent even.

5

So, that morning in 1990, we went downtown alone, my father and I. In the car, a Peugeot 504. Later that afternoon we would be leaving for a vacation in La Serena, and my father needed cash, more than he could take out from an ATM.

'Why did you need so much cash?'

'Because workers were going to paint the house while we were on vacation.'

'And how come we went to the bank downtown and not to the Santander . . . '

'Santiago. Back then it was called Banco Santiago.'

'But why didn't we go to the Maipú branch of Banco Santiago?'

'I wanted to go downtown, I wanted to buy something at a store on Bulnes. A fishing rod, something like that.'

'Why didn't you buy the fishing rod or take out money before the day we were leaving?'

'I don't remember! Maybe I wanted us to go downtown together. It was the first day of vacation, but I still wanted to go downtown, with you. I liked to go out with you.'

Ours was an unnecessary trip, then. My dad parked where he always does, on Agustinas and San Martín, near his office. We went straight to the bank, the branch on Bombero Ossa. While he waited in line, I sat reading in a corner. Suddenly I felt watched or inspected or threatened, and I looked up and caught a young man's blue eyes. A second later, the man had disappeared. As my father walked toward me he was calmly, innocently counting the bills he had just received. I don't know how much money it was.

'Four hundred thousand pesos,' he says, with certainty.

'And how much was that, in today's money?'

'I have no idea. Figure it out online!'

I figure it out online, and it takes a long time: one-thousand-three-hundred dollars, more or less. In five-thousand-peso bills, that I remember.

'Why in fives? I checked online and there were already tens in circulation in 1990.'

'Really? Well, I don't know, maybe they weren't that common. Maybe they were too big, hard to change, the painters needed to buy materials.'

I didn't think the blue-eyed man was dangerous. I didn't believe in the existence of blue-eyed muggers. But I still made a strange movement to warn my dad. And I was annoyed that he was so unconcerned, that he would count the bills right out in the open like that. He handed half the money to me, just in case. He smiled at me first as though approving of my caution, my good judgment. Sometimes, when parents congratulate their children, they're actually congratulating themselves; they applaud themselves for something they judge auspicious or positive, though its merit may be arguable. In this case my caution, maybe my paranoia or fear, seemed to my father like the product of his own virtue.

I remember the weight of the bills in my right pants pocket.

When we came out of the bank I asked him if he thought blue-eyed muggers existed. I was trying to make a joke, but he didn't get it. He said something, I don't remember what. He doesn't remember either.

6

We were on the basement floor of the bank, and we went up the escalator. Escalators made me nervous. They hadn't always, I liked them at first, I sought them out and preferred them, but then I started feeling afraid of that upward entrance, the downward exit. I was too alert to the moment when I had to pick up a foot and reactivate my steps slowly, gradually accelerating. Predictably, I stumbled when I got off the escalator, and that clumsy movement forced me to look backward and then I saw that the blue-eyed man was following close behind us, along with another man whose eyes weren't blue, but brown like mine and my father's, although the two of them did look alike, maybe, I thought later; the blue-eyed mugger and the brown-eyed mugger looked a lot alike, as if they were brothers.

We turned right, intending to go to Café Haití. In a fit of optimism, I thought maybe the danger would end there, and that, like we had so many times, my father would order an espresso and I'd get an almond frappé, and we would return the obligatory smiles of those scantily clad young women with endless legs, whom I looked at with such shame and delight. But the muggers cornered us five or ten steps before we could enter the Haití.

My father decided to do something very smart that at the same time came off as extravagant or ridiculous: he decided to make a scene.

'Thief!' yelled my dad, pointing at the muggers.

'You two are the thieves, you fucking thugs,' shouted the brown-eyed one, pointing at us, and he sounded persuasive.

That's what I myself thought then, in the moment. For a thousandth of a second I thought that the accuser sounded convincing, because the thieves were whiter than us. Or maybe what I felt was the harsh scrutiny of the hundred or two hundred or five hundred people who were out on Paseo Ahumada and who turned to look at us, alerted by the shouts.

The brutal thing about prejudice is that if I had been in that crowd, I would have thought we were the thieves too. Maybe also because I was badly dressed, while the muggers were decked out in sports shirts and colored jeans, which were a novelty at the time. I was always badly dressed. Once a year my parents gave me money to buy clothes, and I spent it on books and a bunch of second-hand clothes that tended to be too big or too small for me, but I didn't care. My father, on the other hand, invested in his wardrobe, but he was and still is an eminently practical man, so he took advantage of vacations to send his suits to the cleaners, and his weekend clothes were all packed for the trip to La Serena. Really, I don't remember what my father was wearing, but I tend to think it was a sweatsuit and sneakers, or maybe that's how I picture it, making it up as I go.

'I don't remember what I was wearing. How could I remember something like that?' he says to me now.

He does remember this phrase:

'You stole my Ray-Bans, fucking bum!'

That's what the blue-eyed mugger said to my father before snatching the green, *Top Gun*-style sunglasses off his face. It left a mark between his eyebrows. A scrape.

'I'm not the thief, it's not true!' My father's cry sounded harrowing and naive.

It would have been easier and more logical for us to run, as if we really were the muggers, but we got caught up in a fight. It wasn't clear who were the pursuers and who the pursued. On the corner of Ahumada and Moneda they knocked us both to the ground, and I got up quickly but saw that my dad stayed down, shouting for them to please let him look for his contact, because the punch had knocked the lens out of his right eye . . .

'Left.'

'OK.'

. . . because the punch had knocked the contact lens out of his left eye, and that was when the blue-eyed mugger went to kick my father while he was down but I managed to get in an awkward hit, like to the back of his neck, and then a kick to the balls, and the blue mugger fell to the ground and I don't know where his presumed brother was – I focused on my father, who was still on all fours trying to find his lost contact, but he never found it because right at that moment a cop put him in handcuffs.

It was a civil policeman, long-haired and wearing a leather jacket. All of a sudden, everything had changed. The thieves had disappeared, and in addition to the civil cop there were two uniformed ones who were arresting my father.

'Motherfucking cops, fucking pigs, you're taking my dad, fucking killers!'

I shouted something like that at them.

'I knew it would all get cleared up, I wasn't scared, but I heard you cussing out the cops and I thought they would arrest you and then I got worried,' my dad told me later.

They took my father away in cuffs, me following along and yelling, and then four or five spontaneous volunteer witnesses joined in.

'The kid is right, this man wasn't the thief, I saw it all,' said a woman around fifty years old, a street peddler, her blanket spread out and full of merchandise.

She was the one who should have been avoiding the cops, but just then she didn't seem to care, and she went with me to the gallery where the cops questioned my father. And she repeated her words several times, furiously, as if her life depended on it. She put her hand on my shoulder, reassured me, told me everything would be OK. My father took out his checkbook, brandished his credit cards. It was a desperate and pathetic gesture.

'Now why would I need to go around robbing people?' he asked.

The cops didn't reply, just shrugged their shoulders and put it all down to a misunderstanding. They did say, though, that he could file a complaint. My dad didn't want to.

I saw the street peddler disappear into the crowd. Later, I walked around downtown many times looking for her. I was sure I would recognize her and be able to thank her, maybe, by buying whatever she was selling, but I never found her.

7

'I never wanted to be a cop,' my dad clarifies. 'No way. What I wanted was to join the air force. But that was impossible, because of my eyesight.'

'OK, I'll change that part, then.'

'And I don't remember writing that poem. But you forgot to talk about how I used to recite.'

It's true. Sometimes, at family parties, after we all did our tricks, he would recite or more like declaim a poem, always the same one, a terrible one.

'It isn't terrible. You don't like it, but it isn't terrible. It's a matter of personal taste.'

It's a terrible poem called 'The Conscript'. Really, I discover now, it's a tango or a milonga that my father recited as a poem. And it moved us. Maybe it took a few years for me to start considering it a terrible poem.

'Why didn't you want to press charges?' As I change the subject I feel like my question is jarring, like it comes off as journalistic.

'Because it wouldn't make a difference, they were never going to find them.'

The brief police interrogation took place in the same shopping center where my father bought his contact lenses. Coincidence. We went into the store, where my father was a regular customer. An elderly man waited on us.

'He wasn't elderly. He was older. Don Mauricio,' my father interjects.

Don Mauricio hadn't seen what had happened, he didn't know anything. We didn't tell him. I was going to, but my father squeezed my hand when I started in on the story. Then he explained he had lost his left contact and needed a replacement ASAP. Don Mauricio told him he could have it the next day.

We left. My father walked quickly, squinting his defenseless eye and leaning on me. He couldn't drive.

'Let's go to the bus stop,' he told me.

'Let's take a taxi instead,' I said.

'You're crazy, a taxi to Maipú? No way!'

'It's on me.'

He looked at me without understanding for around ten seconds. Only then did he remember I still had half of the money in my pocket. As did he – we hadn't been robbed. Just that pair of sunglasses.

I hailed the taxi myself, and we sat in the back with our arms around each other. I remembered another taxi ride, some years before, when we'd also ridden in an embrace. My father had crashed head-on into a truck. It was the truck's fault, it was going the wrong way. One of my father's best friends was riding shotgun without his seat belt, and he was seriously injured. A friend who from then on was no longer his friend.

'That's not true, we still saw each other after that,' my father objects, annoyed.

'But you weren't friends anymore, not such good friends.'

'Those things happen.'

Even though it wasn't his fault, since there was a serious injury, my father had to spend a night in jail. My mother, my sister and I went to pick him up, and we took the bus there but a taxi home, all four of us squeezed into the back seat. He started to talk, and I don't remember his words but he was trying to soothe us, console us, and yet suddenly he began to cry, and then we all cried. We cried for the rest of the taxi ride. Maybe fifteen or twenty minutes.

The Peugeot 404 was declared totaled. And the mark the seat belt left on my father's chest was there for good. Then he bought the Peugeot 504 that we'd left that morning in the parking lot on Agustinas. During that second long taxi ride, we didn't cry.

I think it was quite the opposite, we celebrated the episode as if we had somehow won something. He thanked me many times and then told the story to the driver, exaggerating it a little, as if I'd acted like some kind of Jackie Chan or Bruce Lee.

8

The first time I tried to write this story, I decided to end it with a scene in 1994 or 1995, when I was in college, and my friends and I were at a protest, running away from the cops.

'Fucking cops, motherfucking pigs, fucking killers!'

As I shouted, I remembered the cops taking my father away. My feeling was ambiguous, parodic, combative, excited, all of that at the same time. Me shouting at the cops and remembering my dad, who appeared as a victim but also a victimizer, because he could very well have been a policeman, of course he could have, at some point he'd wanted to be one.

'But I told you, I never wanted to be a cop.'

'But I thought you did. When I was shouting at the cops, I thought they were like you.'

'They're like you, too.'

'Maybe so. We could have been cops, we could have been thieves.'

'No, I've never stolen anything from anyone. And I never wanted to be a cop. Fix that. You said you were going to fix it.'

I don't know if my dad would have liked to see me there, yelling at the cops.

'No, I wouldn't have liked it, but I figured you were out there.'

I never told him – what for? We had enough to fight about.

'True.'

That feeling never went away. At every protest, when it was time to yell at the cops, I remembered my father and felt a turbulent emotion.

I felt it again the last time I was in Chile, in 2019, a few days after the October civil uprising. I traveled on short notice, alone, and I saw my parents and my infinite extended family of dear friends. And with some of them, I went to the protests. And when it was time to jump up and down shouting '*el que no salta es paco*' ('if you don't jump you're a cop'), I felt all of it again. Maybe that time I felt it differently, because in addition to thinking of my father I was thinking of my son, or feeling that I had become my father, and thinking of that future world when my son would protect me and defend me and judge me.

I look at photos from that recent past. There's one of my son smiling with my glasses on. He was obsessed, back then, with my glasses. He'd play at taking them off me and running with them at what was his still very slow top speed. I remember having the thought that I would recognize him in a crowd. I mean: without my glasses on. Because he had hid them from me, and as I looked at his hazy, haloed face, I wondered if I would still recognize him if I saw him in a crowd. And I replied to myself, maybe to put my mind at ease, that I would.

9

'Have you finished making breakfast?' my father interrupts me.

'It's ready,' I say.

We sit at the table. My father, who had breakfast hours ago, will take this moment to nibble on half a bread roll and drink coffee.

'You'll have to start paying me royalties for everything you've written about me,' he says. 'Silvestre, your dad is writing a book about me,' he says to my son.

'I wrote a book too, it's about my dad,' says Silvestre.

'What's it called?' my father asks.

'*Alejandro's Problems.*'

My son loses all interest in his quesadilla with chapulines and tells my father all about that book. It's the anecdote of the moment, he's repeated it many times over recent days, ever more aware of the peals of laughter it generates.

A few weeks ago I spent several days with a fever. Not Covid, but some strange and persistent infection. One morning, when I was starting to feel a little better, my son insisted on staying beside me playing the Covid test game, which to this day is one of his favorites. He sticks his right finger in his nose and looks at it in the light, theatrically, and intones 'positive' or 'very positive' or 'negative' or 'very negative'. That day, out of nowhere, he started to cry. Maybe he felt like I was ignoring him. He leaned his head against my shoulder, but didn't say anything. I think he was somehow imploring me to get better, once and for all.

Then his mother managed to take him into the living room, and that was when he told her about his project, *Alejandro's Problems*.

'What's your book about?' she asked him, dying with laughter.

'It's about Alejandro's problems. Alejandro has a fever. Alejandro spilled a glass of water on his computer keyboard. Alejandro is scared of squirrels. Alejandro lost his glasses. Alejandro can't find his glasses because he doesn't have his glasses. Alejandro's head hurts a lot.'

Now he tells the same story to my father and adds a few more chapters. My dad can't take it anymore, he's almost choking with laughter. Then he asks me if it's true about the computer. I say yes, I'd had to buy a new one. He asks if we're OK on money. Used to be, when he asked me that, I would say in a stoic voice that I was in dire straits, thinking he would immediately transfer some money from my inheritance. But that never happened. So now I tell him everything is under control.

'But how could you let that happen?' says my father, as though to himself.

Spilling a glass of water on the computer, I think, must seem like the stupidest thing in the world to him, the stupidest thing that can happen to a person. But he doesn't say that.

My wife joins in the laughter and the breakfast, then takes my son out to the kitchen garden. Some months ago, when she grew convinced that the pandemic would be eternal, she planted a small garden, and now she's growing chard, peas, onions and basil. I stay two or five more minutes to talk soccer with my father. He says he has to go.

'I'm almost finished,' I tell him.

'With what?'

'The piece I'm writing about the assault. Those fragments I read to you.'

I want him to read the final version. I ask him timidly. I think he's sick of my questions, but I also sense that no, he wants to participate, he likes that I remember that story, this story.

'You want me to read it right now? You think I don't have anything else to do, that I don't have work? I'm up to my neck in work.'

'I'd like it if you read it now.'

'OK,' he says, unexpectedly.

I send him the file, he opens it, and for a second I think he's going to read it immediately, in front of me; that I am going to watch his face as he reads for fifteen or twenty minutes. For a second I think that would be the *natural* thing. But he hangs up, because that is the natural thing.

I wait for his reading, his call, and I'm irrationally nervous. I don't smoke anymore, but I feel a desire to smoke one or two or all the cigarettes I can in the time it takes my father to read my story. But that would add a new chapter to my son's book: Alejandro started smoking again.

'I read it,' my father tells me, finally, half an hour later.

'Did you like it?'

'Yes,' he replies, without hesitation. 'I liked it a lot, son. It's really funny.' ■

LADAN OSMAN
Deep Dream of God (I), 2017

DIARY OF A JOURNEY
TO SENEGAL

Ishion Hutchinson

The day ends with this miracle: a meeting with Ayi Kwei Armah. It is extraordinary how that happened, a sort of epiphanic encounter that explanation flattens. When I was going to Popenguine, it was mentioned to me that an old Ghanaian writer lives there in the village, that he speaks English (of course) and that it would be great for me to meet him. The name might've been said to me, but I didn't register it; the meeting was actually agreed on or was spoken of as likely possible. Still, I wasn't excited about meeting this old Ghanaian writer living in a sea-town village: all my interest was in the sea-town village itself.

On my walk through the village main street to the beach, I remember passing a man in a faded lilac jumpsuit, a perfect cloud or halo of white hair framing his small dark face. The jumpsuit, I thought when I passed him, looked like an astronaut's outfit. We nodded greetings and went our ways. The stay at the water and the cliff, abiding in their healing, kept me overtime, and so I was late in rushing back to the village to meet up with my host for the (possible) meeting with the old Ghanaian writer. Even as I rushed back I stopped at an artisan's shop at the side of the road, an old corrugated-zinc shack with masks made of refuse – iron, bottle stoppers, carton boxes – hanging on the side walls of the shack. I called for the owner. A man, fifty-ish, emerged from the inside. He pointed out that the artist, Mussa, was presently at home, which was a short walk up a dusty and craggy hill next to the shack.

Late to meet the old Ghanaian writer, I went in search of Mussa instead, climbing the hill and arriving at Mussa's yard, which resembled his art shack: litter everywhere, but because of the paintings and masks hanging from his little house and the trees, the yard, like the shack, took on the quasi-sacred feeling I recognized from the yards of obeah man or witch doctors from home.

Mussa was sleeping in a low rugged hammock in front of his house. Cooking utensils strewn around him; a fire recently gone out was still smoking. A puppy was tied next to him with a string. I had to call several times to wake him; when he did wake, he rose and literally unfolded his limbs out of the hammock, so the man who had seemed so small lying down stood as tall as a palm tree in front of me, with the biggest smile on his face. He spoke some English. He invited me into his house, a box structure of one room that had a dirty mattress in one corner and was filled with the scrap material he turned into his art. He worked in this room by a candle at night, he told me.

'Only at nights?' I asked him.

'Only at nights,' he said.

I wondered why, but there wasn't enough language in common between us to discuss it. He showed me the mask he was making the night before, this one laden with rusty keys and coins and bent nails in the mouth holes. 'Beautiful,' I told him, and he touched his chest and said thanks.

We left his room and walked down to his art shack. He opened up the windows and showed me around. Of all the pieces that grabbed me, I kept coming back to a pink-mauve canvas with what looked like a raft sewn from cowrie shells. He told me to rub my hands on the shells. They felt like the welts of an old wound, which was what I was about to say to Mussa when my host appeared in a panic: they had been looking for me to take me to the old Ghanaian writer. Apologizing to Mussa, we left the shop and climbed another small hill to the writer's house.

On the way, my host told me a heartbreaking story. That morning, a friend, an aspiring writer, had taken his life. It was a heavy thing to hear in the sunlight and amid the bougainvillea. He was the most recent in a series of suicides. 'And all so young,' she said. I said, 'I am sorry to hear that,' unsure of what else to say. I thought of a young African photographer I had met in Berlin who, not long after, took his life. We walked on in a silence so deep I didn't realise, shortly after, that we had arrived at the old writer's house.

There was the cloud-hair man in the lilac suit from several hours ago! He offered greetings and water. The space was a large room with low shelves of books lining the walls, airy and bright, a table-tennis table in the center. Books and papers were laid out for us to walk around and browse. I took his greetings, apologized for keeping 'island time'; he was congenial and spoke with a twinkle in his eyes, waving me off and saying that he was glad I was there now.

I went over to the table-tennis table to see the books which were laid out, most of which belonged to the same publishing house and were produced in the same style, so cheaply made that they seemed more like reproductions than books. But then I started to notice that most of them bore the name Ayi Kwei Armah. That was when it struck me. I looked at the name on the cheaply printed books, and then at the old man in the lilac suit, then back to the books. I said, 'Are you Mr Armah? Am I in Mr Armah's house?'

He was as surprised as I was; I walked over to him and took his hands: the myth made flesh, the hands of the very first African writer I ever read, at Happy Grove, and the hands of the man who inadvertently deepened my love of literature, whose writing haunted me. After reading his *The Beautyful Ones Are Not Yet Born*, I refused to touch the railings of stairs and doorknobs for months, so powerfully (and lastingly) he conveyed human disgust. *The Beautyful Ones Are Not Yet Born* was my first African book; the first time I lived with African characters and, in those very young years, the first time I had come to the sense or knowledge that the desperation of poverty, its disgust, was not only the terrible aftermath of colonialism, but a reality (terrible to recognize) common to his world and my own, in so many intimate ways, despite the vastness of space and time between us. Reading that book as a boy was an awakening. I said as much while I shook his hands.

And it was so that I met the old man of that early glimmering of self-consciousness, the old Ghanaian writer in the village by the sea, and it was truly moving.

The conversation was, naturally, about the man himself. His coming to Senegal from Ghana ('snared by a beautiful woman'), and how before that he had decided, when very young, to develop his knowledge of Africa, to, in fact, become African by traveling throughout the continent and residing long term in different countries. He has now lived in many parts of the continent.

The knowledge – of Africa, his knowledge and great passion – began in Egypt. The walls of the room were lined with books about Egypt, ranging from its language to its culture and history. 'No country in Africa,' he said, 'studies in their institutions the knowledge of Egypt. They don't see that Egypt is the source knowledge of all of Africa.' He spoke sadly and slowly about this. You could see the young man he was in the old man he had become, the singular determination to possess something difficult and far larger than could be grasped in one lifetime: that was the drive, to submit to that impossibility and write his way into it.

He had done his work, and continues to. His home, in fact, was a place where village children visited to do 'play workshops' in Egyptian hieroglyphics; he had founded a printing press which made Egyptian-themed children's books; he translated (from the French) massive tomes of out-of-print Egyptology books: there were versions of these, so large and thick, phone-book size, with liners from at least seven different languages (many of which were tribal African) set off in bright colours on each laminated page. The admirable enterprise made me think of the young man's determination which can't – or won't – be met with 'success' in his lifetime, but must be done. The recluse, as indeed he had become, lived by touching the outside while remaining on the periphery (there was early fame with *The Beautyful*, but disillusion followed soon after).

I sat low in my slung chair, looking at him in disbelief and admiration. The head of cloud, the lilac jumpsuit (like an astronaut's uniform), the affable expression on his face, which remained present even when he voiced his failure (not so much speaking of it as failure but with the open admissions that things had not come to fruition or remained small – and yet it was so large an issue, the cradle of knowledge of an entire continent and the world, and he was one of an almost-forgotten minority who was fully entrenched in that knowledge!). He spoke and spoke about himself and his quest for the knowledge of Africa, but he was not self-indulgent or self-involved in doing so. Then he started to ask questions about my life and my work.

My mouth felt dry in responding. If it were just the two of us alone, I would've wept. I spoke to him about home, especially, to my surprise, about the rivers of Port Antonio.

Îles de la Madeleine at dark. The sea at night is a dance floor of occasional foaming white lights cutting thin and broad, horizontal and vertical, so that one feels plunged into a parallel universe of happiness standing before the waves.

The night sea wears a light-feather coat and a scent so dangerous planets cover their noses, but still they bow to the sea. Sea night music: what is the music?

That music is the underbelly of leaves flashing in slight breeze, so that the sound is much more in sight – an acute sound like razor blades thrown on ice – and the mountains making small steps, rocking back in place, repeating and repeating.

The sea at night. Somewhere between Port Antonio and here, Îles de la Madeleine, lie these forgotten (nearly, for fishermen still use them) and never-inhabited group of islands (four altogether): there, rock pools fill with water that looks black and greenish but is as clear as tears; bluffs are whitened by the shit of cormorants and other birds;

the wonderful clear smell of this ancient and renewed bird shit that has the balm scent of salt.

Now I know something else, something about the composition of the sea at night, the dance that lasts into the shimmer of morning and all is full of a settled, coral joy.

D usk. How soft the light falls through the still bright bougainvillea, that, without sun – or rather with the sun so lowered down – they're brighter, bright as the last gasp of coals in a stove, of life beginning as it ends. The soft dusk with its sounds. I can hear the movements of things and register them as familiar – not familiar: intimate. As now I hear the clatter of utensils from the building next door: I hear and see the hand pulling the kitchen drawer out and grabbing the well-used silverware and allowing them to clang on each other, for the sheer reason of their sound, just the delight of doing so, letting the forks and spoons and knives take claim as living presences in the house. I hear voices. Bubbling up they waver, their tones carefree. The fast but pronounced lilt of mixed languages. Now a woman's voice – her bright laugh – fills the dusk. A child's squeal follows. More laughter, this time in unison. Is there a party of people drinking – sitting, I imagine, at a low table (hands reaching for drinks and peanuts) – over the wall by the pool? I am writing this at the guest house, in a lounge chair by the blue-and-white-tiled pool – a single swimmer in the water (cloudy with chlorine) moving waddlingly without haste. Noises from other apartments: a radio playing consistently the same jingle between the news and a talk-show program.

Somewhere else, the loud creak of a door as it opens, and is then slammed shut.

The light, along with the tender softness I feel so at ease in, am embraced by, is cool: cool not because it is dusk but because it is light as a breeze. You can touch this light as you would a breeze; it touches you. There's a transfiguration in it, or about the way it sinks, risking final extinction, the heart beating faster because dark is now imminent and you're already missing the light: you'll miss this light so terribly! For it embodies you as a substance of touch. Touching light. That's fair and not bad.

To sit here in all that's happening, that has happened, to be with what will continue when I'm gone, this gentle dusk which if I had to trivialize and risk giving it a painter's name – or rather a painter's colour – I would say Constable, the happily melancholic light like alchemized hay, so not quite yellow: the light at dusk is more a low-wattage peach, blown to its brightest glow. Light you must strain your eyes in so as not to see but to feel who is touching you. My grandmother's eyes are like that.

A change of swimmer. An old man, well, not old, early sixties, brisker than the previous (younger) swimmer, splashing as he does laps, diving to the bottom of the pool, resurfacing and spurting out water.

Lights are coming on in apartment windows. The dusk has reached its final moment. A thought comes to me that the soft light of dusk could be so soft or is softened because the extraordinary swirl of dust in the heat of the day, tempestuous and unrelenting, has quietened and transformed into dusk. Dust to dusk. One is being touched (this is a partial possibility) by luminous dust particles . . . the final moment of dusk! Exactly now the evening's call to prayer is struck up. And there is another sound to this light which makes at least one thing absolutely clear: pay attention, give thanks.

I will go to pick a flower of the bougainvillea by the pool, in this last light, to put in the jar of tears and to add to the veritable garden I've collected on my table. Branches, twigs, leaves, flowers – the little things I've taken from every place I've been so far.

O f Joal, only the road to Joal. Not the sea. I was hoping very much for it. So be.

E arly waking (all mornings have been an early rise) and quickly packing for Saint-Louis. Morning is made tropical by the various sounds of birds in the mango tree in the courtyard of the guest house. The mango tree has the broadest leaves I've ever seen on a mango tree, almost the size of the leaves of breadfruit, but slimmer and waxier, and of a denser green. I sip coffee under it. Few guests are about. Guests here come from nearby African countries, and those I've met, invariably, are here for one conference or the other. Yesterday I met a guest from the Gambia at breakfast, who told me he was in for some sort of editorial conference. He gave me his card (he had noticed me reading and thought I was a writer). Breakfast: baguette with tomato and Cheddar and goat cheese; I eat little of it. My food is the morning and the journey to come.

There is here a sadness not easy to grasp but that can be seen: such squalor in every nook and cranny; the garbage lining the sea and frothing up on the shoreline. Not just garbage in little puddles but vast, thick amounts bubbling up in great heaps. And the stench. The smell like many dead things commingling. That stench, the fetid horridness of it for several miles, that stench goes to the deepest recesses of the hurt I feel and the sadness. One word bears the weight: colonialism. But I'm coming to think of the word as naive, not as an excuse, but certainly as a myopic and even arrogant justification of the rabid dumpsite the sea around the island of Saint-Louis has become. It's a shame. A terrible shame because of how people live – at least from my first impressions – with and on the garbage: at ease, comfortable. I don't mean there's no sense of outrage – I heard that bitter outrage later – but there's a living with this burden, nonchalantly, to the point where it is not even avoided, or perhaps that is impossible to do. People trail in the horseshit from the many horse buggies around and trail that shit into buildings; droplets of feces on the ATMs or in cafes; the children about – so many kids! – racing and playing on the steaming heaps of garbage; adults dumping more dump from apartment windows; flies on everything, everywhere.

So the ugliness of this assaults and is noticed before the beauty. The ugliness, this kind, is the direct resonance of an abiding other.

The worst ugliness, which is colonialism's ancient twin, imperialism – its invincible, destructive power touching everything on the landscape. Before long, in one stunning instance, I'm to see how its gnashing and gnawing maw eats up and regurgitates the lives of the most vulnerable members of the society.

But now, the beauty, for it is staggering once seen.

Where the beauty is to be found (besides in the degradation itself – it stretches the civic imagination to see the rows of fallen buildings, many ruins leaning into each other so they form one, seamless unending line along the waterfront – the former 'glory' of the colonial architecture) is in the people. Let me not forget the great look of kindness in each stare that held mine from the very moment I entered the town's walls.

That kindness was magnified in the eyes of an old, retired fisherman I met on my second day.

I had gone walking early in the morning to the traditional quarter of the fishermen in Saint-Louis, an old part of town lined with innumerable colorful wooden fishing boats, many no longer seaworthy, beached and rotting on the jetties and on the sea walls dividing the ocean from the land. I was standing in the cool of the morning on a part of this sea wall when the old fisherman came up and stood next to me. He greeted me with a smile. I greeted him back, and he immediately realized I was a visitor and didn't speak any of the local languages. He spoke enough English for us to get on. He invited me to walk with him through the fishermen's quarter. He would show me life there. I agreed, and followed.

How I first arrived at the fishermen's quarter was by crossing an iron bridge which connected the old, colonial artery of Saint-Louis to where the fishermen lived: the iron bridge, I came to realize, was a symbol of a deep division between the area of the fishermen's quarter, Black and unruly, and a certain idea of Saint-Louis still ingrained in a French colonial mentality, rather than a connector. On both sides of the bridge children were scavenging and playing in the squalor of bilge water. I saw a boy piss and then scoop up the murky water and wash his penis with it. I had seen a man doing the same thing the previous evening. Rotten pirogues were beached on both sides of the bridge. In the guts of these discarded pirogues, trash, all trash imaginable: here the discarded or the disregarded mingled with filth beyond comprehension. Across the bridge, on the side of the fishermen's quarter, were market streets: tumbled-down shacks streaming with people and goods. There was a monument at the small roundabout to First World War soldiers. An inscription in French. Two figures whose race I couldn't tell faced each other.

Beyond that was the sea wall. The strong, unremitting smell of urine and filth at odds with the strong, healing smell of the ocean. Black muddy water with trash at my feet. I looked long out to the sea in the early cool of morning, the waves large and rough. Turquoise water. A few pirogues in a lovely symmetrical line, barely perceptible, in the distance. Even far away, their bright colours and painted effigies could be seen: reds, yellows and greens. They brought to my mind Indigenous American canoes. As I was thinking this, the old fisherman appeared next to me. He was not that old, actually, about sixty, but he had been retired from the sea for some years now, as he told me later, and that's what had made him an old man. With no work, he said with a secret twinkle, I do nothing but survive.

Our epic walk through the fishermen commune, where families have lived for centuries in more or less the same condition, was heartbreaking as well as marvellous. The houses, crammed so closely, were made from cinder blocks. I could glimpse courtyards in most, some with a waterpipe and a trough where animals were tethered. People were doing morning chores: women washing in tubs at their front door, others cooking on stoves in narrow passages. Food peels, chopped-up vegetables and parts of fish thrown in heaps, squelchy underfoot. Children everywhere, running out of the narrow passages, dragging animals or gathered in groups of three or more on stairs. Later I found out that five years ago a tidal wave destroyed the main public school – and other municipal buildings, including the main clinic in the fishermen's quarter – hence why so many kids were about during the day. We turned into another passageway, this one much wider, and almost clogged with animals – sheep mostly – and mongrels being driven by young boys. We exited the passage and witnessed, wondrously, an old man sitting on a crate with a gigantic pelican in front of him, which was eating from his palm. After every mouthful or so the bird cleansed its great beak on the man's neck. The retired fisherman told me that the pelican was the man's protection. I asked if he meant like a watchdog. No, he said, like a spiritual protection, like a gri-gri one which could never leave the man's side, which he's responsible to take care of as it takes care of him. 'Is it always with him,' I asked, 'like bedtimes too?' 'Yes, yes!' he said.

We continued through the rows of houses. The cacophony and rubble caused my mind to flash to the old sugar-cane barracks I knew in Saint Thomas, a place I only ever truly walked through once or twice (the ground of mixed cane ash, marl and mud), and where I had felt, as a child, a sadness and a grief in my chest I didn't know how to utter. That returned as the fisherman showed me the grimed and caved-in living quarters; and it was when he took me into a maternity clinic, where heavily pregnant women were rolling on beds and stretchers pulled into the passages, moaning in terrible pain – the strong scent of disinfectant stalking the corridors – it was then that I asked him if we could please go to the water. He understood. But I think he wanted to show me the ward as a point of pride, show me that the women had a place (perhaps since the destruction of other clinics) where they could go and be taken care of . . . but we left.

We cut behind the maternity ward along a trail, where a medium-sized mosque lay in shambles. We walked towards the sea. The fresh air cleared my nausea. We walked in silence on the sand. I was happy, quite glad to find such a clean stretch of beach. The fisherman pointed out to the sea and explained: Mauritania that way, that way Spain, and that way to Brazil. I asked him where he had gone. He said Mauritania. Good fishing there. (This was true, and later I discovered fishing was the cause for much tension between Senegal and Mauritania; Senegalese fishermen, apparently, routinely break off-season fishing laws in Mauritanian territory.) He told me about fishing – his excitement as he spoke make it hard for me to follow what he said, for he slipped almost exclusively into Wolof. But it was such an intense, moving pleasure to listen to him talk and gesture toward the sea. He grasped my shoulder and said – this I made out clearly – that he would take me to meet his 'amigos' where we could have tea. (I thought 'amigos' a strange word for him to use, and guessed perhaps that his friends were Spanish.) 'My amigos he is a good, good man, and now like me no more fish any more. But he is big boss, my amigos.' I understood 'amigos' then was one person, his former patron, and that 'amigos', in that sense, was like 'patrón' or 'jefe'. I agreed to go, and we moved further on in silence a bit, the beach beginning to change. First there was a dead, bloated sheep on the pathway, as if to presage the tyrannical level of garbage we were soon to trek through, and then a veritable slum yard appeared, stretching for miles along the shore. I didn't know how to ask him why this level of garbage was on the beach. Was it simply a dumpsite? To ask would be disrespectful, I thought, as if I were insinuating that he had something to do with this municipal nightmare.

We walked, picking our way through the debris. Then, as we neared the Muslim cemetery on a raised hill by the beach, I saw a most touching, beautiful thing: an old man praying towards the sea. His frail body rippled in the wind; he wore only a dark wrap around his privates; his chants carried on the wind and around his ankles the waves came and circled, creating a large ring that seemed like his own radiance. Occasionally he lay down flat in this circle. The water covered him. He rose up with a sudden spring, flashing water off his body and brightly coloured necklace: he chanted louder each time, spreading his arms. After one of these dips he walked out into sea: the waves were powerful and pounding and once he was waist-deep, in a move splendidly agile and age-defying, he leaped in the air, curved into a perfect arch, and dove into the sea. It was like watching a dolphin for a moment, the water glistened off his body while he cleared the sea briefly as he rose into the air and fell back without a splash into the water. For several moments he was gone. I looked wildly around for him; the moment stretched, and I panicked, but just then he rose again some distance from where he had dived into the water. He swam to shore with ease. He stood back in the same position he was in before, and began to chant, spinning as he did until he moved out of the range of the surf, and then he began walking on the dry sand towards the township.

We moved on, and approached the cemetery: sea-blasted, the gravestones bleached white by salt. There was something solemn about passing the rows of haphazard graves, just the two of us. The graves disappeared, and about half a mile on an area appeared that turned my stomach: hundreds of rotten wooden racks filled with women working in complete muck, salting sardines. Countless black and grimy fishes gutted and thrown into the mud. The scent was horrific, an overpoweringly rancid stench, and I didn't know how any human could bear breathing it for long. Still, I wanted to enter this complex. The retired fisherman didn't want me to at first, but eventually we climbed the grating. Up close, the putrid smell was like burning in the nostrils. Heaps and heaps of sardines with their heads torn off on the ground, and on long slatted tables their bodies were spread for salting by women working in groups of three and four. Some of them turned to greet us. They were splattered with the guts and blood of the fish, the bottom of their faces wrapped with rolls of cloth. We threaded through the middle of the operation – the tearing off of the heads, the gutting, the slapping down of bodies, opened up to be salted. As we passed a group of these women, one of them looked up to greet us and I stopped in my path, my knees shaking: she looked exactly like my mother. I gave the Wolof greeting back to her, tears in my face. I didn't know what to do; she walked over and I could see the flowery pattern of her headdress beneath the remains of fish and dirt. I embraced her and asked the retired fisherman to tell her that she resembled my mother. He did, and she spoke to me, pulling down the scarf from her mouth. 'She is saying,' he said to me, 'that she is your mother and you're welcome here.' All of that, in her voice, was much longer. She held me the whole time she spoke. When she released me, I couldn't go on any further down the salting line. I thanked her, and we climbed back down the little hill to the beach.

On the beach – garbage and more garbage – we walked for about twenty minutes until we drew near to a township of cinder-block buildings in various stages of incompletion, and there, the fisherman told me, his amigos lived. At the edge of the town there were many old and new pirogues beached on the sand. There was something equally prosperous and ruinous about the area: unpaved streets with little corner shops in front of which men gathered, some talking and others simply standing in the shade. He asked me to wait under a tree by a brand new pirogue – the paint was still wet on it – until he returned from letting his amigos know we were visiting. I sat on a rock and leaned on the tree.

Behind me, the sea. The breeze carried many different scents from the apartments and voices. I almost began to drift off to sleep, when just then a boy in a long white tunic came and stood in front of me. He seemed to be around twelve, his head shaved close, which might have been fresh given the way he kept rubbing at it. I greeted him, he smiled and said nothing, but walked up to me and touched my hair. He took one of my dreads out from the knot I had my hair tied into, and pulled it gently. Just for fun I said 'Rasta', and he said it back and added 'Burna Boy', the name of the dreadlocked Nigerian Afrobeats star. I smiled and asked, 'Naka-nga sant?' 'What is your name?' But before he could say anything the retired fisherman returned, and the boy strolled off.

The retired fisherman said the amigos would see us. We walked through a dusty lane bordered by high-rises, and crossed over onto a wider road into an area studded with lower houses. We walked up to one with a finished ground floor and a half-built second floor. We entered the tiled, spacious ground floor, and took off our shoes. A woman in a long, shimmery blue-and-white frock escorted us into a living room. It was a surprisingly small room, given how large the house seemed from the outside, and how spacious the hallway we entered from was – but part of the room's smallness was due to how it was stuffed with two large, dark, oversized sofas (both still wrapped in cracking laminate plastic) and several brown barrels, one with a flat-screen TV set on top of it. The woman pointed for us to sit down and called out to the room adjacent. Two girls entered, both in crinkling rose-coloured dresses, and came up to the woman who whispered something to them, and then they all left. Two boys entered, greeted me and my guide and sat on the floor. Both immediately started playing with their mobile phones. I asked the old fisherman who these people were. The woman was a wife (the second wife of two, I believe) of his amigos, and the girls and boys were his youngest children. Where was the amigos? He turned the question to one of the boys. They had an exchange. He then explained that his amigos was, in fact, having a nap. He added that the amigos was busy all day, seeing to the making of new pirogues to add to his fleet, so he was tired, and I was meant to understand that the nap – supposedly undertaken in the ten minutes between the retired fisherman leaving the amigos to come get me – was a show of his status. I suggested we leave, as I didn't want to intrude, but he said he was sure the amigos would be with us shortly, and we could only wait until the nap had ended. It was while sitting there that I began to understand the caste complex of their relationship, and later when the amigos entered I understood how much lower down on the caste ladder the old fisherman fell. While we waited, the old fisherman spoke loudly about the goodness of his amigos, his voice cast in the direction of a locked, light-vinyl door to the left side of the room. After a couple of minutes of this, the amigos opened the vinyl door and entered the room. He was one of the tallest persons I've ever seen in my life, well over 6'5", even though he was slightly bent – the slight bend making him appear even taller. You could tell he was very skinny under his pristine white gown. He had a gentle, very black face, and small eyes that were groggy with sleep. The face looked so familiar to me, but I was blanking on where I knew it from. The old fisherman rose instantly and clutched the amigos's hand, going through the greeting ritual. The old fisherman seemed to have shrunk in size next to the amigos. The greetings over, he pointed to me and I stood and greeted him in turn. He smiled at me and said, in English, 'You're welcome here.' (That was the extent of his English, so everything said between us after was communicated through the rapid tapestry of simplified French, English, Wolof and the gestures of the old fisherman.) He held my hand a while, covering it with both of his palms. I was more or less staring up at his chiseled face, the cheekbones high and prominent. Then it struck me: his face looked very much like the cart driver in Ousmane Sembène's great short film, *Borom Sarret*. I was obsessed with that film for many years, watching it sometimes four times per day. The poor, nameless cart driver entered into my dreams. And now, here he was (I fooled myself) in the flesh. As soon as we sat down, his daughters re-entered with a tray of tea, which the boys took and started to pour. Only the retired fisherman spoke; the amigos smiled placidly at him and then at me. When the tea was passed around in the frothy shot glasses, he said we would drink this round and then leave for his fishing hut on the sea. The room was very hot. The boys were sent to get the hut ready ahead of the amigos, the retired fisherman and myself. Two gulps later we exited the house, taking the same route we had just come down back to the beach. When we got to where I had shaded under the tree, the retired fisherman told me the newly built pirogue I had observed was one of the amigos's new fleet. We stood admiring it, the retired fisherman knocking on its side and prow (the word *Zola* blazoned in red on the tip). The amigos stood back from it, smiling, arms folded behind his back. The new pirogue conveyed more of his status: this one was for his youngest boy, who would have his own crew for the sea. All of his elder sons were now bosses of their own fleets – how many elder sons I didn't get – and even with all of his boys plowing the sea, he still had other men working for him. The retired fisherman used to be one of these men. As I learned later, it seemed the fisherman depended on the amigos for handouts since his retirement, in order to survive. I learned too that the retired fisherman had a daughter, nineteen, who worked at the same dreadful sardine-salting mine we had walked through an hour ago. It must have been too painful for him to tell me when we were there, standing in that high stench. ∎

NIGEL HENDERSON
A man crossing Bunsen Street in Bethnal Green, London, 1950
Tate

GHOSTS

Adam Foulds

M y great-aunt, Esther, visiting the world's first settlement house in Whitechapel, briefly left the tour group to walk through a doorway and out onto a balcony from where she looked down and saw people in historical dress performing, as she thought, some kind of play. Turning to call her husband to come out to see, she found herself in front of a wall where there was no doorway, though the guide later confirmed that there had been one there a century or so before.

My grandmother thought this story was typical of Esther, who, as far as my grandmother was concerned, made too much of her quite commonplace faculties. Esther played the piano and wrote her own songs. The first time Esther met her future daughter-in-law the dark-haired young woman wore a wedding dress and veil of effulgent white that disappeared with a blink to be replaced by her actual clothes. My grandmother was a more down-to-earth person. She could not sing or play an instrument. When she was a child in the East End of London, she saw people in drab and dirty old-fashioned clothes among the crowds. These people looked unwell or hungry and they seemed to be trying to get the attention of the passers-by, pulling at their sleeves, running after them in the crowd, beseeching postures of begging and so forth. One of them caught my grandmother's eye, stood still, looked directly back, and vanished.

My elder sister, aged about three, ran in from the garden to tell my mother that Uncle Harry was out there, sitting in one of the chairs, smiling at her. (I've always had a very clear mental image of this encounter, though obviously I didn't see it myself: Harry's white shirt with a vest visible beneath, and braces, and the sun shining mildly on his brown, bald head, his kind, heavy-featured face communicating friendliness and peace.) My mother began to explain that he wasn't out there and at that moment the phone rang in the hallway with the news of Harry's death.

A few weeks after my grandfather's death, my father was in synagogue opening the ark that contains the Torah scrolls when he felt my grandfather grab his arm. My grandfather went to synagogue all his life. Those familiar with these places, unobtrusive buildings on ordinary London streets, will be able to imagine the comfort he felt inside their modest renditions of divine grandeur – wooden benches, a table of prayer books with donors' names pasted inside the covers, velvet drapes in front of the ark and over the lectern with silver or gold embroidery forming Hebrew words or stars of David or a little lion of Judah, jingling silver bells on the handles of the scrolls. He knew the services by heart and could attend them in a revery or while having a conversation with someone. And so it is not surprising that he would appear there of all places.

If my grandfather wanted to say something to you, he'd first grasp your forearm to get your full attention. 'Here,' he'd say, or 'Here, listen,' or 'Here, I want to tell you something,' or 'Here, pass the salt would you.' He liked salt and horseradish. He gripped, he hugged, he had rages and moods. His eyes would sometimes brim with affection. In synagogue, he was often called up for the mitzvah of opening the ark and this is why, my father thought, he grabbed him at that moment. It was unmistakable, he said; it was absolutely him.

I myself have seen certain things. They were less plain, less external, more like thoughts dropped into my thoughts from elsewhere. Once it was the face of a friend who'd just died, smiling, radiant, entirely free of pain, the centre of a vast, unreasonable reassurance. He stayed with me, in my sight, for a while and then disappeared. Afterwards, I could picture him again but I could no longer simply sit and look at him; he had gone. I resort to this memory at times; I rely on it, though in my fear, my doubt, it shrivels away to nothing.

For reasons of work and marriage, I live now on another continent, far away from all these people, in an unrelated world. Nothing here refers to them except me. Outside, snow falls, slowing the traffic. Faces appear and disappear behind masks. At night, the numbers of dead crawl across the bottom of the television screen. And if I could, I would step right through these walls. ■

THE RIGHT TO INTIMACY

Raphaela (Rosie) Rosella

with Dayannah, Gillianne, Kayla, Laurinda, Mimi, Nunjul, Rowrow, Tammara, Tricia and our families

Introduction by Nicole R. Fleetwood

T hough we have never met, Raphaela Rosella and I are tethered by carceral archives and a devotional love to family, friends and neighbors who have been swept away, disappeared or who are no longer alive due to the prison industrial complex. Both she and I reside in settler colonial states; she in Australia, I in the United States. For many years we have both worked within distinctly different, yet similarly marginalized, working-poor communities on the visual record of the carceral state and its impact on intimate life. Half a world apart from each other we have been amassing a range of personal images, letters and ephemera, alongside punitive mandates and carceral state records, which reflect both the violence of prison and the ways that criminalized and imprisoned people forge and maintain relations of love and care. As activists, artists and scholars of 'carceral aesthetics', we build new modes of belonging in collaboration with people impacted by prison, ways of imagining otherwise.

Rosella's photo-based projects grapple visually with what American literary scholar Saidiya Hartman describes as 'the power and authority of the archive and the limits it sets on what can be known, whose perspectives matter, and who is endowed with the gravity and authority of historical actor'. Focusing on criminal indexes and state records of arrest, custody and confinement, Rosella interweaves photographs of women in her intimate life – relatives, lifelong friends – with documents of state bureaucracies that criminalize them and leave them vulnerable to further punishment and marginalization.

The images of women that appear in Rosella's projects are not only photographs she located in state archives, but portraits of women in her life whom she has witnessed entangled by carceral bureaucracies, some never to recover or survive. The projects amount to counter-archives of state records, and are co-created by Rosella with Gillianne, Mimi, Nunjul, Rowrow, Tammara, Tricia and other women in her life who are subjects of these records.

Rosella, who is of Italian-immigrant descent, grew up in a lower-class family in a small town in Australia, where daily contact with the police was the norm. 'It's a heavily policed town, known for its alternative and open drug culture. The word "taxi" would echo throughout the main street each time the cops were spotted. It was a way we all looked out for each other in resistance to the relentless police presence that routinely harassed and surveilled our small community.'

At an early age, Rosella knew that she wanted to be a photographer. While in primary school, she saved up for her first point-and-shoot camera. By high school, she was involved with a community arts organization documenting her own community, as well as other marginalized peoples and communities in Australia. She became the face of the organization, and was an internationally known artist by her early twenties. During this period, she photographed portraits and environmental images of communities in distress, like her award-winning portrait of a young girl, Laurinda.

Rosella is now ambivalent, even critical, of these early works, stating, 'When you're learning photography it's instilled in you that you should try to win awards to elevate your career. The most sensationalised imagery and content were consistently winning these competitions. But that didn't feel right. So I've pushed back against this in the kind of imagery that I make. Sometimes I just need to put the camera down and be present as a sister, family member or friend. And sometimes not every aspect of our lives is for an audience to see.'

After fifteen years of working in collaboration with this organization, strictly in the documentary tradition, Rosella grew increasingly concerned about the power dynamics of the archive, her practice and the organization that was facilitating and promoting the work.

'I recently left the organization because I started questioning whether their projects were really moving beyond collaborative rhetoric. I started with them as a young, vulnerable teenager, and so did a number of my co-creators. We started as participants together. In recent years I noticed power dynamics were playing out in the work that I was making for the organisation. There was a big issue where one of my co-creators wanted to withdraw consent from one of their projects, and they just weren't listening to her requests . . . This has led me to grapple with several questions within my personal practice; how can I work in a relational way without unconsciously forcing power over my co-creators, especially those positioned across varying states of unfreedom? I've now spent over fifteen years co-creating photo-based projects alongside several friends and family members from my childhood and adolescence. This has resulted in a co-created archive of photographic works, moving image, sound recordings, state-issued documents, love letters from jail and ephemera. So, who controls our co-created archive? These are the questions I'm looking at within my PhD.'

Co-creating with the women in her life, across several communities, evolved as a practice of refusing state narratives, resisting documentary objectification and counter-archiving the images and stories that mattered to them. 'I have several co-creators, and some are heavily involved at times and sometimes they step back. But it's definitely a relational process – I've been looking at relational ethics and those kinds of concepts. And I came across your work and "carceral aesthetics" just made sense, especially in terms of navigating carceral bureaucracies and surveillance.'

One of the first iterations of this co-created archive emerged as the series *We met a little early, but I get to love you longer.* Motherhood starts at a young age for the girls in Rosella's community, including herself. In her early thirties, Rosella is a mother of three. Her twin sister became a mother at nineteen, and her step-sister had five children by the age of twenty-four. *We met a little early, but I get to love you longer* served as an opportunity for Rosella and the women in her life to self-document their experiences of mothering and care by combining existing state records and images with their own photographs and writings. Because young mothering is pathologized by the state as the source of a myriad of social ills, these personal archives claim this space as one of deep longing, loving and hope.

In their effort to explore how personal archives function within this ongoing installation, the co-creators made the multi-channel video installation *HOMEtruths*, combining phone recordings from prison, super 16 mm film and images captured from Facebook and Snapchat accounts. 'Home' is a fraught concept for the dispossessed and imprisoned – those whom settler-colonial states attempt to eradicate – and so the installation is ephemeral and evocative, not of specific locations but of states of non-being and non-belonging.

Juxtaposed are two images of a young woman. In one she poses at a three-quarter angle, sitting consciously for the camera in dark light with a device tucked inside her bra. In the other she floats in muddy water, her hair a puffing cloud.

The tender and mighty practices of women's love and commitment to each other resonate through this evolving archive, as does the expanding reach of the carceral state. Rosella acknowledges that she did not set out to do work on incarceration, but the prison industrial complex and punitive governance more broadly find their way into so many aspects of the lives of poor, single and Indigenous women that it became unavoidable. A co-created archive on the lives of young and poor mothers is also an exploration of criminalization and the state violence waged against them, currently reflected in their series *You'll know it when you feel it.*

Included in the series are letters from prison, some written by incarcerated mothers to their babies. There is an emotional tenor of effusiveness in letters from prison. They overflow with desire and longing.

The word 'love' is pronounced repeatedly, alongside hearts and smiling faces, handwritten emojis, emotive doodles.

Here time is not linear, but cyclical, though this might seem paradoxical given that many of the women are sentenced to hard time. What I mean is that Rosella's projects make intergenerational connections that interweave the past, present and a future potential. A four-set of institutional photos of infant twins nestled together – presumably Rosella and her sister – appear near another four-set of photographs of a newborn wrapped in a blue crocheted blanket. In other photos, a young boy raises his head to the ceiling and wails. The partial nude bodies of a mother and young child showering together feel off limits; the child looks out from the shower. The mother's back is to the camera.

You'll know it when you feel it unfolds an entanglement of poverty, hyper-criminalization, drugs, pregnancy, gendering and communal mothering. Rosella says, 'I was looking at motherhood, and what was expected for us as young women growing up in low socio-economic communities. And I started realizing that the project was about the cyclical nature of poverty and the burden of low expectations. I never imagined my girlfriends would be incarcerated. Growing up, it was usually our boyfriends who were locked up. Just like I never imagined they would be incarcerated, I never intended to document our lived experiences across carceral divides, but here we are.'

Growing bellies and the scarred bodies of pregnant moms – Rosella's co-creators – appear throughout the archive. Babies are signs of hope for mothers struggling with addiction and criminalization. The mothering bodies appear as transformative nurturing embodiment, as well as also being the subjects of criminalization and state control. Drugs alter a feel or a state of being. They also cause states of suspicion and surveillance, hypervigilance and paranoia.

Amid this beauty and devastation, this endurance and love, the state's narrative intrudes through language that frames the movement and possibilities of the women who are the subjects/subjugated: 'Instructions to plead not guilty' and 'Release Certificate'. Co-creators respond to their carceral biography in turn by taking state documents and culling them, revising them and amending them for other narratives.

One of her collaborators, Tammara, who is now deceased, began redacting her prison documents and other state forms that recorded the forced removal of her children from her care. Tammara reveals the errors and contradictions found within her records. Her redactions obscure key details, turning bureaucratic forms into art objects, acting perhaps as a way of reclaiming the privacy and autonomy stripped from her by state authorities.

You'll know it when you feel it documents the interminable wait under penal time. One collaborator journals the daily grind of nowhere to go and nothing to do while in rehab:

Day 3

Was going to leave at
Lunch then went to
my bed and fell
asleep till 7:30pm
Really want to leave
But no where to go 😣

These photographic and textual interventions are akin to the artistic collaboration between American artist Titus Kaphar and American poet Reginald Dwayne Betts, whose exhibition *Redaction* at MoMA PS1 in 2019 incorporated portraits of criminalized people and redacted legal documents that tethered them to the state. These practices demonstrate a growing transnational awareness of the dominance of punitive governance as a way of life in settler colonial states, and how interventions like the work of Rosella and her co-creators point toward the possibility of art facilitating practices and communities of resistance.

Rosella and her co-creators curate an archive of pain, of endurance, of love and belonging, of alienation and disconnection. Amid the cascading array of image/text in *You'll know it when you feel it* is a modest school photo of a young Rosella. She looks out in a way that seems to embody her ongoing collaborations, inquiring, with an awareness of what it means to be shaped by institutional narratives and an insistence to be recognized beyond those limitations. This insistence and spirit of inquiry guide her work, and the way she continues to honor the presence of women in her intimate life. ∎

To my One and Only baby Boy Gage,

hello, its mummy or as you know me as (Tommy Mummy)!!!
How are you? i hope you'r "New Mummy" is treating you good.
you would be 3 years old now, and to think that DOCS Took you from me when you wer only 3 mths old. :(
I am Just wrighting to you to say how much i LOVE and MISS you!!
it hurts So Bad to think i may Never see you again But i refuse to think that and i say i WILL see you again. It may Not be as soon as i would Love But One day you will be in my arms again. and when you are i WILL Never Ever Let Anyone Take you away from me Ever Ever again.
I want you to know that i Love U and you have a baby sister Now. her Name is Tamika and We would Love it if you Came and stayed with us on the Beach and we could go Swimming. That would Be so fun Hey my little man. I ♡ U   I ♡ U   I ♡ U
Love U alwayz Mummy Tammara xoxoxo

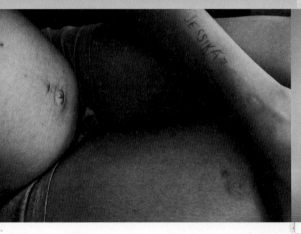

QUEENSLAND POLICE SERVICE

STATEMENT OF WITNESS

Occurrence #: ▮▮▮
Statement no.: _____   Date: 07/01/2014

Statement of
Name of witness: ▮▮▮, Tammara Lee
Date of birth: 18/04/1988   Age: 25   Occupation: Unemployed
Police officer taking statement

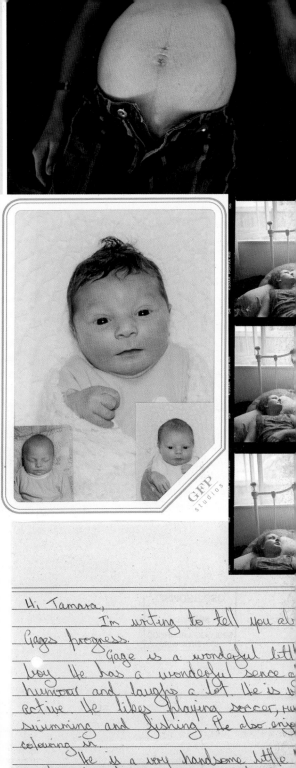

ue Bum Bum Jessika,

...i, I miss you like crazy.
...y I have not been in your
...ew years but I wish I have.
... have been spoilt by your
girlfriend!!!
...n some photo's on facebook of
...I have you grown,
...r photo when you lost your
...all I could do was wish I was

...own house now and hope that
...would come and stay for atleast
...weekend or even One week.
...can show you how much I Love U...
...a baby sister who lives with me,
...Tamika. I got her Name
...x of My Name and yours.
...& Jessika.
...you to Know how much I Love
...ould go to the End of the Earth
...d Do Anything To hold you in
...ain.
..., I miss you, I MISS U!!
...Alwayz AND forever
Tammara. x♡x♡x♡x

KANIS
UCC

Hi, Tamara,
        I'm writing to tell you ab...
Gages progress.
        Gage is a wonderful littl...
boy. He has a wonderful sence o...
humour and laughs a lot. He is v...
active. He likes playing soccer, run...
swimming and fishing. He also enjo...
colouring in.
        He is a very handsome little...
He has big brown eyes and lots of...

...of age And beginning to EAT solid Foods Such as Farex And Puree aswel. oh and begining to 'coo' she hears me Calling her name when i turn up and Whik up to her and she instantly starts Smiling and Trying to call me back. she is getting so big.
When i Called Mum a few days ago to speak to My brow old 'Tamika' And Mum Said that tamika is playing up on her Big time and needs me to try funkin IDATP As Quick as i Can And get up to Grafton prison so She Can Bring Tamika to visit Me And For Me to Try Reason With her to be good For 'Nanny'!

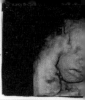

17-5-17

Hi, how have you been? Me, Not so good?
I am writing to you From The Emu plains Correctional Centre in Penrith, Sydney.
I have had 2 more babies since 2011. So i have now got 5 beautiful children out there Somewhere in this world.
I had a boy in march 2016 and named him Braxton (AFTER BRAXTON HICAS (FAKE LABOR) who WAS Removed A short time AFTER Birth FACS have placed him with his older Brother "Gage" in Foster Care, And The Carers have already Adopted "Gage" And changed his Name, And Are already the primary Carers of Braxton until he is 18years and Will More than likely start trying to adopt him as well ;
And i had a baby Girl who i named "kaiya" Sence i have been in Gaol Too.
It turns out So Far that i am Not EVEN Classed as suitable to go to Jacaranda which is a Mothers And childrens par of the gaol To EVEN, have a slight chance to have my babies in My care.
I can Not EVEN Believe how bad my Life has become.
Will i EVER Have an opportunity to show that i Can be a Responsible mother?
I am 17 months clean From Drugs And Am Still Deemed unfit to Parent.
Am i not worth the chance to EVEN TRY An Prove Myself? to Show that i CAN Do IF I CAN LET MY PAST GO, Why CANT THE

From Tammara

Order for assumption of care and protection of child or young person in hospital or other premises

Children And Young Persons (Care And Protection) Act 1998
Section 44

Name of Child or Young Person: BABY MACROKANIS
Date of Birth: 19.03.16
Age:

above named child/children and/or young person/s who is/are currently in premises known as LISMORE BASE HOSPITAL

...are suspected on reasonable grounds of being at serious risk of harm, and the Director-General is satisfied that it is not in the best interest of the child/children and/or young person/s that the child/children and/or young person/s be removed from the premises in which he or she is currently located.

...fore, the Director-General has assumed the care and protection of the child/children ... young person/s under Section 44 of the Children and Young Persons (Care & ...ction) Act.

...child/children and/or young person/s may not be removed from the premises described ...e without the written approval of an authorised officer.

...44(2) states that this order does not cease to have effect merely because the ...children and/or young person/s is/are transferred to different premises.

...ns for the assumption of care and protection of child/children and/or young person/s:
  a) drug use of mother
  b) unstable living arrangements
  c) concerns mother may leave hospital with baby
  d) unstable mental health

Signature of the Director-General: Position: CASE WORKER
Contact No:
19.03.16

...see the attached information sheet: Information for parents and carers following the ...al of the child/children and/or young person/s by the Director General

---

28.5.16

To Rosie
Thank you So Much for the letter That you sent to Me.
...y Time here at fresh hope has been pretty awesome experience.
...Still Cannot Believe how good i have been doing here.
...fit in pretty well And have been earning a lot that has been So So So beneficial To Me
...have started to have phone Calls with Tamika, i wrote a Letter To baby Braxton That is up on my wall ...the Moment with a printed Copy ...a photo of Me holding him done in Black + White.
...Get to go And Visit him Just yesterday! And he is now in size ...o But he is doing So well. A ...few days ago we got to go ...room horses to Session We do ...lled "horses + healing" ...hat was So So Awesome.
...t to Call + Talk to Mum, Tamika, ...ek + Rose on Mothersday And also ...st to call Meeks on her B-Day.

6.5.16

To My Beautiful Baby Girl Tamika.

Mummy has Been having so much fun on her holiday But is always Thinking about her Sweet Little Bubbles Girl.
I am looking forward to our First Phone Call and for you to Come visit. Would you like that? I But you would. Guess what, i Live with alot of animals on a farm.
There are chooks, ducks, Geese, Dogs, Cats, Kittens, Sheep and a Baby Lamb.
oh mummy Nearly forgot, There are also Some Guinea pigs and a Horse. There are 4 other Mummys and Their Beautiful children and Babies aswell. One of the Mummies Keeps Calling Me Tamika. I Do Not mind as that is your name And I miss you Like Crazy.
My Bedroom is all Done up in Red, I have a Red Bed, Red Curtains, Red Towels, Red Flower, Red Flower Vase, Red Candles + All my Blankets, pillows + Bedside Tables Are all Red.

I Love you So Much xoxoxo
Love Always MUMMY

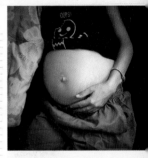

LBH.
Sue ___ midwife - ___
Signed Consent Form for "Drug Testing
filled our Birth Registration paper
Baby Braxton.

Contact = with "URA".
  2 x 1hr per week. Visits. - u
  starting visits Friday

Any sms/calls MUST Be Replie from urcela. Re- Baby Brax Vis

Manager Jan ___ - family

urcella on Leave - 22 April - 11 may

mum. charli + meeks to Attend meeks + charli Can start Visits wh work out. Times.

find ou
Place h
(same

Section 90 for Return of Baby.
Restoration To Mother.

NIMBIN CENTRAL SCHOOL KINDERGARTEN 1993

FRONT ROW:
SECOND ROW:
BACK ROW:
Tammara

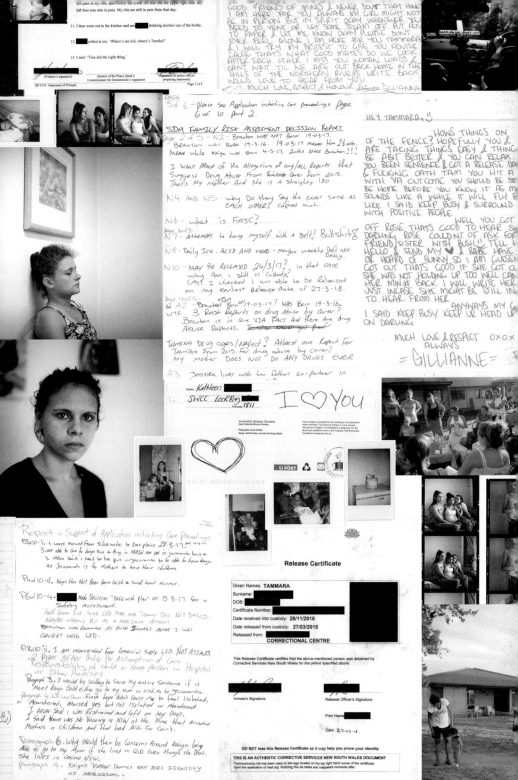

You Rosie You Made My Day!! I'm Getting Out On The 1st of July 5 Days Before My Birthday Lol, I'll Might Come Visit or You Come Visit Me? I Live Next Door To Laurinda In Dingwall And Tycannah On The Corner Lol.

And Yes Pls Send Me That Necklace Or Ring The Jail Ahol Ask IF Its Possible That You Could?

25.12.16
I ROSIE !!   PAGE 1.
        HOW ARE YA MY GIRL? WELL I HOPE THAT
S LETTER FINDS, YOU & THE FAMILY IN THE BESTEST
SPIRITS & A "BIG" MERRY XMAS FOR TODAY & WISHING
ALL A HAPPY NEW YEAR... WELL WHERE DO I START
ST OF ALL I AM TRULY SORRY I'VE LANDED MYSELF
A PLACE LIKE THIS "JAIL" TO ALL THOSE WHO MATTER
T TO ME ESPECIALLY 'MY CHILDREN PLEASE ROSIE MAKE
E THEY NEVER FORGET HOW MUCH THEIR MUMMY LOVES
M & HOW MUCH ALL THEIR LITTLE SOULS MEAN THE WORLDS
ME !!!! AS LONG AS I LIVE I WILL NEVER LET MYSELF
 DOWN TO THE TIME I LEFT THEM & NOW WITH ME BEING
NCARCERATED TIL GOD KNOW, WHEN I AM ON SOME PRETTY
ED UP CHARGES (SERIOUS) AGG BRE TWO OF THEM
RECKON THEY GOT FINGERPRINTS ON EXTERIOR OF BOTH
 DS I DON'T KNOW ATM WHAT I'LL BE LOOKING AT BUT
AL AID SAYS IF CONVICTED I WILL BE LOOKING AT 3 YEAR
 THE BOTTOM STRAIGHT IF FOUND GUILTY BUT FUCK IT I'M GONNA
T THE CHARGES ALL THE WAY NOT GOING DOWN WITHOUT
IGHT BUT IN THE MEANWHILE I'VE APPLIED FOR SUPREME
 BAIL HOPEFULLY I WALK ON THAT IT'LL BE STRICT
 BUT FUCK IT I WILL HAPPILY DO WHATEVER THEY SAY
 I DON'T WANNA COME BACK TO THIS SHIT HOLE EVER
N BUT TO HIT THE NAIL RIGHT ON THE HEAD
ARE SURE I BE WALKING ON SUPREME COURT BAIL
RITY $$$ & I NEED ATLEAST ONE STARTING $300 to
 TO THROW AT JUDGE TO GIVE CONFORMATION THAT
NT GONNA FUCK UP WHILST ON BAIL IF I GET BAIL
 MOST PROBABLY WONT BE LOOKING AT THREE YEAR
 SENTENCE SO I AM PRAYING DAD, JES, AUNTY MON &
NONE ELSE WHO IS WILLING TO PITCH IN RUN THE BALL UP
SE CUNTS HAVE ME PINNED RIGHT UNDER THE THUMB FEEL
 I CANT DO SHIT ONLY TO SIT IT OUT THATS WHY I

QUEENSLAND POLICE SERVICE
Domestic and Family Violence Protection Act 2012 Section 106
POLICE PROTECTION NOTICE
RESPONDENT
AGGRIEVED
RELEVANT RELATIONSHIP
CONDITION
COOL-DOWN
NO CONTACT
COURT APPEARANCE
ISSUING POLICE OFFICER
363 George St, Brisbane. Brisbane Magistrates
The Gap

(SORRY ITS TAKEN TOO LONG HAHA TO FINISH JUST STARTING 2nd PAGE?)   16-02-2020 Sun
                                                                      11-02-2020 Wed
Hey Rosie,♡   31-01-2020 Fri

        I HOPE THIS LETTER FINDS YOU IN
BEST OF HEALTH & HIGHEST OF SPIRITS...

WELL ROSE WHERE DO I START MY GIRL I FEE
LIKE THIS ROLLAR COASTER OF A RIDE I'VE BE
ON FOR THE PAST FIVE YEARS AIN'T EVER GO
COME TO A HALT... FOR THESE LAST FIVE YE
"WOW" WHAT A FUCKING WHIRLWIND... WELL
COULD SAY MORE THAN A WHIRLWIND" FUCK IT'S BEE
SELF DESTRUCTION AT ITS FINEST & TURMOIL ASWELL
AS ONE HELL OF A RIDE AND JUST AS I SIT BO
AND THOUGHT IT COULD NOT OF GOT ANYMORE WO
SER THAN IT IS... WELL WHAT CAN I SAY I'VE GO
NO-ONE ELSE TO BLAME BUT MYSELF BUT IT IS WHA
IT IS... THE FAMILY GET TO BURY MY GRANDMOTHER
WITHOUT ME!! YOU SEEN FIRSTHAND HOW CLOSE I W
WITH NAN 'SHE WAS MY QUEEN & MY EVERYTHING S
RAISED ME TO BE THE WOMAN I AM TODAY, EVEN
THOUGH SHE WAS STUCK IN HER WAYS I KISSED T
GROUND SHE WALKED ON I LOVE HER WITH EVER
INCH OF MY HEART & SOUL... SHE IS GONNA BE V
MISSED & I'LL CHERISH HER MEMORIES ALWAYS & FORE
AND WILL NEVER EVER FORGET HER BUT ROSE PLS D
BE SAD I'M GONNA BE OKAY REMEMBER IT IS WHAT
IS AND SHE BROUGHT ME UP SO STRONG & I KNOW D
DOWN SHE IS BY MY SIDE ALL THE WAY UP THERE
THE DREAM-TIME SMILING DOWN ON ME PAIN FREE
& HAPPY AND KNOWING THAT KEEPS THE WARM FIRE
BURNING WITHIN ALIGHT NO MATTER HOW HARD LIF
WILL GET I WILL NEVER LET IT GET ME COLD...
WHAT DONT KILL ME WILL MAKE ME STRONGER

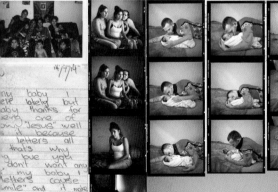

14/7/14
my baby I
 lovely but
by thanks for
ing one of
my "Jesus" well
   because
 letters all
 that's why
 love you
 don't want any
 my baby I
 letters cause
 smile" and it make
 swear I wish
 good I swear
y baby "haha
 think they mgt
 rs just to be
 kathleen ♥
ats all
our on my
 baby my baby
 I'm so inlove
 tell like this
 of my kids
 that's the feeling
 think you know
 want this more

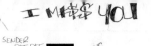

...other day from work the high count 2 hours from you any phone
yet send me some pics of all the kids for my wall please
love you my sistah write back ASAP
...ya more madness [love] you [love] Robyn_____ xx

SENDER
DEE DEE
MIN # _____ 2 WEEKS
IN SEGREGATION SEGRO
Wellington c/c

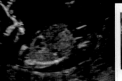

II Kath

& R

TO MY SISTER ROW ROW
2 MY SISTER ROW.
NEVER IN A MILLION YEARS DID I
THINK YOUR WORDS COULD EVER MAKE
TEAR UP THE WAY YOU DID YOU LITTLE
IS. YES I FUCKING CRIED. IM SHATTERED
NOT GOING TO BE OUT THERE BEFORE YOU
ME HERE IN THIS POXY JAIL MAKEN SHIT
UP ON MY OWN, YOU ALSO REALLY TOUCHED
SPOT IN MY HEART TO THE POINT IM MY
YOU FAMILY NOW. I RUN WITH YOU AND
RUN WITH ME, YA GET ME WE 2 OUT NOW
MEANS THE WORLD TO ME WITH EVERYTHING
SAID TO ME IN YOUR LETTER, ROW MY
... YOU TRULY ARE ONE OF A KIND AND AS
WE WANNA RUN AROUND LIKE SOLDIERS
DON'T THROW YOUR DREAMS AWAY FOR
... YOU ARE AN AMAZING YOUN INDIGENOUS
... WITH SO MUCH POTENTIAL, YOU COULD
PURSUE YOUR DREAMS AND WHAT
YOU HAPPY, YOU WERE AND ARE SO PROUD
STORY IS ALL OVER THE WORLD SO GO BE
OUR BEST MATE WHO NEEDS YOU, GO TRAVEL
WORLD MY SOLDIER AND SHARE YOUR STORIES
J THE WORLD WE CAN STILL KICK IT
FOREVER GOING TO BE MY RIDE OR DIE
...ER
... MY, THIS MY,
THIS MY MOTHERFUCKING CELLY
REMEMBER PRIORITIES TAKE TIME
OR YOU KNOW MATTER WHAT SISTER
OW YOU OUT FOR LIFE
CHIDDY CHIDDY BANGS COME OUT
PLAY IN TIME Respect

TRICIA
... PAGE
TWO
TROY
HUGH
WILLIAM

...T OUR MOKO TOO TRICIA! FUCK DAT AY? SO ARE WE GOING
T FAMILY PHOTO WHEN OUR IS BORN? ... RECKON WITH THAT MOTHA
... LD BE POSTING, MY MONG UP FOR THEM AY? TRICIA WHEN YOU WRITE
... THAT CAN YOU TELL ME WE NEED OUR OWN WAT IN DRAWS? MY
TV FOR OUR ROOM, MY MONG UP FOR PHOTO AY? TRICIA ALL
HAS BE DOESN'T? MY WE ALL KNOW I SHARYN? ... ROB MOANING TOO
... WE ARE? WANT TOO WORK? SO WHOSE/BRODA? OR ARE THEY STEADY N
... ME KNOW, I HOPE THEY STAY THERE WITH YOU BECAUSE THESE CAN
... LOND, MY WE KNOW BECAUSE WE ARE GOING TOO GET
... AND IF MY NEED TIME TO HELP AY? MY WORRIED MY BABY?
... 20 WKS NOW? LAST PHOTO? I GET OUR MY AND 13 WKS AGO?
HAD A LOOK AT MY AT 20 WEEKS PLUS? ... I GET MY ARE LOOKING
MISS YOU TOO MY BABY

TA MY ARE THEY WON AND I LOVE MY FOR THE WORLD? I AM
... I HAVE MY IN MY LIFE AND HAVE SOME BEAUTIFUL HEART TRICIA
... MY WHEN I GET MY IN READY TOO TELL MY HARDEST TOO BREAK MY OLD
I WANNA BE THE BEST MAN/ DAD TOO MY AND OUR BABY? I'M DOING
... AT MY RIGHT, I'M READY TOO KICK DA AROUND BUT I'M TRYING BECAUSE
WANT TOO TREAT MY LIKE I DID, THAT WAS BULLSHIT AND, I AM
SORRY FOR THAT MY BABY? MY WON MY? I LOVE MY
BABY? TRICIA, I WANNA MISS YOU THANK MY AGAIN FOR THAT
... I GOT FROM MY? THANKS BABY MY WON YOU BABY? MY WON YOU
... MY MEAN THE WORLD TO MY?, I CAN'T WAIT TOO KNOW MY WON
LOVE MY, MY BABY? I WANNA KISS, HOLD, TOUCH, TASTE, MY AND
MY WAIT? TRICIA ARE MY HAPPY THAT MY ARE GOING TOO BE A MUM/
... MY PLO? I PROMISE THAT MY ARE GOING TOO BE A BEAUTIFUL
MUM AND OUR BABA IS GOING TOO HAVE NOTHING BUT THE BEST IN
HOW MY BEST? I LOVE IT FOR NOW, LOOK AFTER YOURSELF I
... AND MISS MY RUB THY BELLY FOR MY PLUS MY BABA AND KEEP

MY BEAUTIFUL BABY
PAGE
ONE
(28th OF MARCH?)

HELLO THERE MY BEAUTIFUL BLACK QUEEN! TRICIA MY ARE MY QUEEN, MY ARE THE
BEST THERE IN MY MY TRUST AY, IM SORRY? DAMN AND STRESS AT MY MY
BABY? I WISH? WANNA COME HOME?, I KNOW MY TRICIA LOTA NO. I KNOW MY
LOVE ME, TRICIA MY QUEEN? I CAN'T WAIT TOO KNOW MY KISSES? I NEED, MY
BABY? I WISH? WANNA SEE? FUCK DAT AY?, I RECKON WITH MY AY TOO
IS TOTAL BROWN INSIDE MY AND, I CAN'T WAIT? KISS MY TAKE TOO
MY THE PRINCESS, MY BABY IS ON TOP OF THE WORLD! MY ARE HAVING A
BEAUTIFUL MY FIRST, I LOVE YOU TRICIA?, SO MY BABY IF THEM ULTRA SOUND
PHOTO? AIN'T GOOD, BUT MY CHOSE OR BUT SEND THEM ONES TOO BEAUTIFUL! THEY
ARE GOING TOO BE BEAUTIFUL ANYWAYS MY MY BABY? SO WAT IS OUR BABA
NAME? GOING TOO BE?, I WANT HER NAME TOO START WITH THE LETTER T?
BUT IF MY WANT TO NAME HER AFTER ANOTHER THING IT'S ALRIGHT? BUT
I LOVE YOU MY BABY

WITH HER FIRST NAME? BECAUSE IM PUTTING MY MOTHER'S MIDDLE NAME IN
THERE?, ALRIGHT? SO IT WILL BE (RODE-DAWN) BUT IF MY WANT TOO NAME?
HER SOMETHING ELSE? WAT AND THAT WANT MY MY? KARLOKA? MY
THAT IF? SOMETHING LIKE THAT AY/ MY BABA? WHEN MY WRITE MY A LETTER
TELL THAT NAME MY HOW MY ARE GOING TO SPELL OUR BABA NAME, ALRIGHT
MY SEXY BABA? IF THAT IS THE NAME? WAT MY HAS SETTLE, THEN WE SHOULD
PUT RODE-DAWN OR DAWN ROSE? AS HER MIDDLE NAME? WAT MY RECKON MY
BABA, I LIKE THESE TWO NAMES OKA, TYEISHA OR TYEISHA BUT I DON'T
KNOW ABOUT THE SPELLING TYESHA / TYIESHA RODE-DAWN-WHITTEN LET ME KNOW
WAT MY THINK PLUS MY BABY? TELL ME THE NAME? MY HAS SETTLE (KARLOTA
RODE-DAWN WHITTEN) THEN MY AROUND WHAT MY ARE MY BABY? WRITE BACK!
THANK PLO? IM OPTIMISTIC/ HAPPY OF OUR BABY NAME?, I MEAN WHEN THINKING
OF OUR BABY? NAME? MY KNOW? WAT I MEAN TRICIA?, AND WHEN MY WRITE
BABA SOUND THESE PHOTO OF OUR BABA AND OF MY MY MY BABY BECAUSE
THAT? THIS SOUND HIM, I CAN SEE MY SEXY QUEEN AND (FINGER CROSS?) MY
BEAUTIFUL BABY MY HAS? PRINCESS MY WON YOU

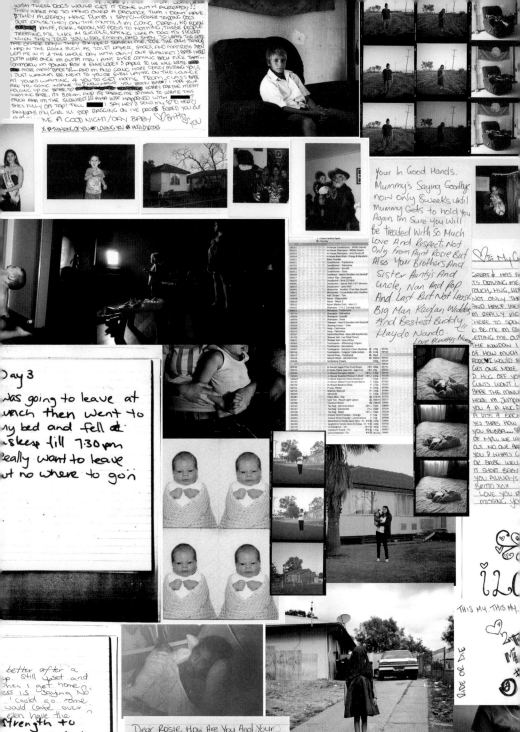

WISH THESE DOGS WOULD GET IT DONE WITH ALREADY!! THEY WANT ME TO HAND OVER A PACIFIER THAT I DON'T HAVE & THEY ALREADY HAVE DUMB I SAY... POWER TRIPPING DOGS OUT CAUSE THEY ON THE ROADS, I'M GOING CRAZY, NO FORKIN KNIFE, FORK, SPOON, NO ACES TO NOTHING, THESE PEOPLE TREATING ME LIKE A SUICIDE, EATING LIKE A DOG ITS FUCKED WHEN THEY TOLD YOU, LISA, EMMA AND CHU... THE FORK THE ONLY THING I HAD IN THE ROOM SUCH AS TOILET PAPER, SHOES, AND MATTRESS BEN LEFT ME IN IT 4 THE WHOLE DAY WITH ONLY ONE BLANKET! BABE I NEED OUTTA HERE ONCE IM OUTTA MAN I AINT EVER COMING BACK FUCK THAT... TOMORROW IM GOING ASK 4 ENVELOPES 3 PAGES SO WE WILL WRITE... MORE NOW! BABE SO... AND IM ALSO GOING MORE CRAZY MISSING YOU I JUST WANNA BE NEXT TO YOU OR EVEN LAYING ON THE LOUNGE AT YOURS WAITING 4 YOU TO GET HOME, MEAN, I... BABE ARE YOU GOING INSANE TO? YOU HAVE YOU... HOLDING UP OK BABE I SEND MY LOVE... SORRY FOR THE MESSY WRITING BABE, ITS 8:00AM AND ITS TAKING ME 30 MINS TO WRITE THIS MUCH PARA I'M THE SLOWEST... HAHA WTF HAPPENED WITH... SHES FULLY OFF TAP! TELL ____ I SAY HEY I SEND MY SO TO HER!! ANYWAYS MY GIRL ILL STOP RAGGING ON I'VE PAGES BORED YOU OUT OUR... LIVE A GOOD NIGHT/DAY BABY ♡ BRITTO ♡ YOU

THINKING OF YOU # LOVING YOU # MADD XKISSES

Your In Good Hands. Mummy's Saying Goodbye now only 5 weeks until Mummy Gets to hold you Again Im Sure You Will Be Treated With So Much Love And Respect. Not Only From Aunt Rosie But Also Your Brothers And Sister Aunty's And Uncle, Nan And Pop And Last But Not Least Big Man Kaylan Wilder And Bestest Buddy Klaydo Nando
Love ALWAYS Mum

Day 3
Was going to leave at lunch then went to my bed and fell a... sleep till 7:30 pm really want to leave but no where to go in

...better after a ...p. Still upset and ...hen I get home ...ss is saying No ...I could go home ...would come over ...gelen have the strength to ...yone not to ...wer & offer me ...an tell a couple ...that's it!

Dear Rosie, How Are You And Your Beautiful Family Going?? Thanks For... The Photos Beautiful, Made Me Cry... Looking At My Babies, I Miss Them So So Much Not Bearable To See There Pretty lil Faces Lol, But other then that I Get to hear There lil Voices ♡ Wow A Big Congrats To You Carlos, João And Mymi On The Pregnancy

Is My...
Great & Has F... Is Driving Me... Touch, HUG, K... Not Only Th... AND HALF WE... IM REALLY NIC... HERE TO SPA... O BE ME IM SU... ETTING ME OUT... THE WINDOW I... OF HOW MUCH... RODENI WOULD... GET ONE MOR... 2 HUG OFF YO... CUNTS WONT L... BABE THE MINU... HERE IM JUMPIN... YOU & A HU... & KISS & EACH... YES THATS HOW... YOU BUBBA... OF MYU, WE WI... OUT NO ONE AN... YOU & WHATS 2... OK BABE WEL... IT SHORT BAB... YOU ALWAYS... BRITTO XOX... LOVE YOU &... MISSING YO...

THIS MY. THIS MY.

ME...
...
RIDE OR DIE

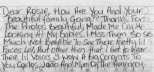

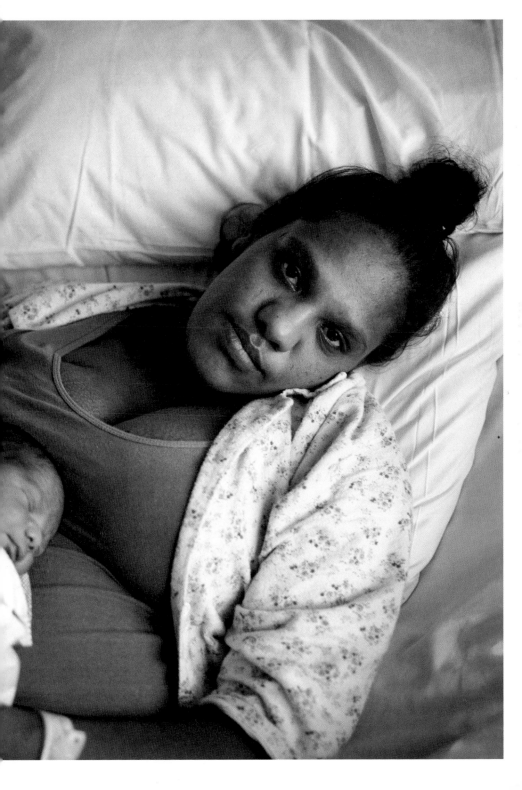

CATHERINE YASS
Corridors, 1994
Tate/Catherine Yass

NATIONAL DRESS

Rebecca Sollom

The Queen was homeschooled and the government, some years before, had settled my parents and me in a flat not so far from the Palace. To be her classmate you filled out an application form, and after that there were many interviews and different types of test. My father took me into the city on the bus five days in a row to sit them while my mother was at work. My parents tell me that it was my idea to apply but I remember it differently. I was a nervous child, even if I hid it well.

The results arrived by post in a real envelope, on real paper. My parents sat at our small, chipped, white dining table, and took turns reading from the document. It was a morning near midsummer but the light in our kitchen seemed thin to us. The sun in this country has nothing to it, no heat. In truth, I did not remember the country we came from, I had been too young when we left. But I believed my parents when they told me the sun here was false. My mother watched my father read, and then the same but in reverse; all the while, neither looked at me. As a unit, they went into retreat. Bewilderment, and silent pride. Like they had outdone themselves, and would never need or dare to guide me ever again, as if they might just ruin their own good fortune if they tried.

My acceptance into the Palace school was no surprise to me. It wasn't the tests that made me nervous, but the footage. I hadn't seen it yet because my parents were worried it would upset me, but everybody else I knew had. When adults watched they cried afterwards, including the President, who often screened the footage before making a public address. *That poor girl*, is what my parents called the Queen. *And she was only three years old*, they would say, shaking their heads.

This was the country we had come to.

I was her classmate for a year. That was the year we were ten, and then eleven – the Queen and I. It was already the seventh year of her enduring reign. The seventh year of our President's, as well.

W hat can I tell you about those days? If I tell you she was lonely, I tell you very little. And yet the whole place was a ship that was listing to her. We were captives, we sensed it immediately, the nine boys and girls with her in that class. We knew this without telling each other so. Certain words and topics were forbidden to us when she was present, words and topics relating to those events that had been captured in the footage. But despite that, a sense of death you couldn't escape. You felt it when you entered. I did not know how much she remembered of what had happened seven years before, and I did not want to find out.

Each morning it was the same. Waiting by the gates. Walking past the facsimile guards in their white-and-navy uniforms, their guns held high across their chests. Then through the scanners, and after that, if it was a broadcast day, one of her minders would come to straighten your clothes and smooth down your hair. The minders were interchangeable to me, even though some were men and others women, some dark and others light, some young and others old; they had an expression in common – taut, responsible concern. As you made your way to class along the musky parquet corridors, any minder you passed would smile. Their smiles were unyielding, like the wood. In response I kept myself very neatly arranged. My spine, my hands. You couldn't help it. The place felt like it held you.

The paintings hung on the walls were there to be ignored, but walking past them every day I had chosen my favourites. One was a vast scene: children, dogs, shot pheasants; silken men in buckled shoes, frozen in exaggerated motion. In the background, Doric columns and a moody sky. The frivolity against the menace made me tingle. The other of my favourites was smaller: a portrait of a woman and a man. The woman's dress was yellow and spectacular. I liked the man's face, but the woman was so ferociously unattractive, so doughy and unformed, that I admired her.

When you reached the classroom the Queen would be waiting, at whichever desk she had chosen, often beside a window. The classroom had no paintings in it at all. Occasionally, a teacher would pull the shutters closed and project a picture onto the white wall – a map, perhaps, or a diagram. The rest of the time we looked at our own screens. The teachers changed regularly, like the Queen's minders, rotating so often that it was our habit to simply call them *teacher*.

I did not try especially hard to grow a friendship with her. I had the idea, perhaps learned from my father or mother or perhaps from a book, that she would like me better if I did not capitulate to her instantly, and of course very quickly I observed how she treated those who did. When I arrived, in the final days of that summer, she seemed especially close to two of the girls and one of the boys, with everyone else, myself included, held at a certain radius of indifference. But the following week I heard her ask the boy what he was doing, standing next to her in line; hadn't he figured out from the way she kept her back turned to him that he should find someone else to bother now? And later, in the dining room, I saw her laughing at the boy, whispering behind her hand and pointing. When I asked a long-plaited girl, later, as we left the Palace together, she told me that the boy was a great athlete, a fierce competitor. She predicted he would leave soon nevertheless; and it was true, he did.

This girl had been in the school longer than most. Three years. Since the beginning. She described her parents as friends of the Royal Family. Or, as she put it, the Royal Family that was. She had three siblings in regular school. They lived on one of the islands to the south of the capital, and she stayed during the week with her aunt, who had an apartment in the city. Every day after school, the long-plaited girl said, her aunt would sit with her and they would discuss, in some detail, every moment of the day she could recall. That was her secret, she told me. How she'd survived so long. Would she tell her aunt about this conversation? I asked her. She laughed. Of course she would. When the long-plaited girl approached the Queen, she often lowered her eyes. My *darling*, this girl would call her, like she was the Queen's grandmother. She was very gracious. I noticed her body tuck under itself a little when the Queen was close by. This seemed to happen without the girl even noticing.

The broadcast days were once or twice a week. People had an appetite to see her on the screen. On some of these days, cameras so discreet we didn't even notice would record short clips of our activities in class. The clips were put out in the evening, so that the public could enjoy seeing her live a normal life. At other times, the broadcasts were more staged, and occasionally, for these, the President joined us. We went along with whatever the Palace had planned, though it exhausted us to know that everything that passed between us would eventually play out before the cameras. The fragile allegiances, the little cruelties and negotiations, all on display. Those who had lasted the longest at the school, I observed, were the ones who were most circumspect during the broadcasts. For example, the long-plaited girl always took a great deal of care to keep a respectful distance from the Queen in front of the cameras, safely beyond the reach of any but the most subtle signals of rejection. She would relinquish her status and position in a self-effacing way. Apparently, she was inured to the advantages closeness to the Queen might give her.

Like everyone else in the country, my parents and I watched the Palace broadcasts at home together those evenings they were on. But they did not ask me for details. So, from the beginning, I decided to hoard them. In any case, it was inexpressible; life in the Palace school did not belong in our small flat. That listing of the ship, I asked myself, at our chipped, white table? Never that.

In those days I still played chess, and it was over a game that the Queen and I first spoke directly. We played on a board built into the top of an antique table. The table sat by a window, which looked out on the parterre gardens, in the small, quiet room adjacent to the classroom. I had to tell her what I liked, she said. I told her I liked chess and she said this didn't count because it was old and dead, and I said that if it was old and dead then I liked it that way. I can't imagine where this courage came from.

Did I want to know what she liked? Did I want to guess?

What first came to my mind, I am ashamed to admit, was jewellery. Her many polished stones lay somewhere below us in vaults, although I had noticed that on her wrist each day she always wore a simple beaded bracelet, surely worth nothing. Her clothes were aggressively plain. When I ventured nothing, she said that she had realised she was like an actor, and that's why she liked the actors in films and on TV. She said this sotto voce. She didn't like films and TV for the stories, she liked them for the actors. 'I didn't know there was a difference,' I said, 'between those things.' 'Of course there is,' she said. She told me that when she watched, she looked through the story, *past* the story, for the person who was acting, and she said she liked the bad actors, not the good ones, because the good ones didn't show you much about themselves, whereas the bad ones were always just themselves no matter what they did.

At home I was not allowed television or films, except for the Palace or news broadcasts, and, occasionally, documentaries. As I told her this, the pleasure of difference I had always felt for that reason, even at ten years old, slipped aside for a moment. She made me want to watch more television.

'I like actors our age best,' she said. 'I know more about child actors than any other kind.' Her eyes were large as she said this, and at times they would go glassy and flat, whether to conceal or to protect, I was never sure. It would often precede those times when she began a spell of behaviour her minders labelled 'unacceptable', at which point they would intervene in some way to contain or avoid it. On occasion, during a lesson, she would stand up and begin circling the classroom tables in her usual slow walk; everything held in place until she returned to her seat. Other times, she would stand at the window and simply scream, her face pressed against the glass, the window shut, until a pair of minders came, took her arms, and placed her on her seat again, or else removed her from the classroom. A boy asked her once why she couldn't go to boarding school; he himself had been at one, for a short time, and he said it had been fun there. 'Because there isn't one that's safe enough,' she told him. 'And besides, I won't go. Can you imagine it?' We had all glanced at one another; we couldn't.

Now, she was bouncing her knees up and down and had a bishop in her mouth. I sensed that her eyes would not go glassy and flat this time. This time, I thought, I would be able to stop it coming to that.

I put my fingertip on a black square. 'You should put that there,' I said. She asked if I was sure, and I understood that she was giving me the chance to change my mind. 'Of course I'm sure,' I said. 'Don't you believe me?' She said she didn't know. 'That's fine with me,' I said. 'We haven't known each other very long, after all.' I watched her face pause, and then assume a softness.

'You should put that there,' I said again. And she did.

The following day was the first that she sat next to me in the dining room. She gave no explanation. It was not what I'd expected. Suspicion, of course, from the others. Perhaps it was simply that a vacancy had arisen. But I imagine she liked that I did not pursue her. I had then, and I still have now, an ability to hold myself in silence, to be quiet and still in my resistance, and I suspect that she liked that about me. Later she said that she could see me in a show as the quiet friend, the loyal friend, who is hiding something desperate. She said she couldn't tell whether or not I would be a villain in the end.

I t was her letters that made the difference. To both of us. She chose the day of the President's first visit that autumn to give me the first one.

That smile the President has – it was just the same then as it is now. Close up, that smile blinds you. When he arrived we pushed our desks to the walls and pulled our chairs into a circle, his among ours, and he pulled her onto his knee. She might have been one of his dogs. He was not shy with her at all. Her smile, as he lifted her, was fixed. The minders and his entourage were smiling too. His sleeves rolled up, like a doctor's. The broadcast camera was already running.

By that age she had already gained a lot of practice. If she was anxious or unsure, she never showed it. Never in front of a camera. She was trained like a professional. She spoke effortlessly, clearly; her consonants were crisp, as an immigrant's like mine could never be. She never looked into the camera, unless answering a question put to her by an out-of-shot presenter standing beside it. On this occasion neither the President nor the Queen looked into the camera, but only at each other. The President asked her what she had been studying this week, and she began to talk about a book that we had read in class. Her reply sounded spontaneous and natural, but I had heard a minder help her to prepare the afternoon before.

He kept his arm around her all the time they spoke. Eventually he took it away, and she slipped from his lap and returned to her own seat the moment he did. After that, he swivelled round to look at me. For a moment I felt blinded again, like I might fall. When he shook my hand, his grip was firm but his skin was very soft. Everywhere, the strange, strong scent of his cologne.

'Welcome,' he said. 'Welcome to this great country. What do you like about it best?' It was difficult for me to answer, because this country was the only one that I remembered. 'Snow,' was what I finally responded, and he laughed. 'Snow in the capital isn't real snow,' the President said. 'If you want real snow, you'll have to travel north.' One day I would, I told him. I tried my best to match his smile but couldn't. All the children sat still in their chairs as he spoke to me, and the Queen gave me a look reserved for amateurs. The President continued. Did I like the Palace school? Was I enjoying the great honour of learning beside our Queen? 'Yes, very much,' I said, copying her consonants. And was I doing my part to take care of her? Here, I only nodded that I was. I confess that I was scared to give him more. I saw her blink at him, her eyes flat and shining. Then she turned away.

That afternoon, after I had already put on my coat, I became aware that she wanted me to approach. We were in the corridor, alone, out of sight of anyone. She took a letter from her bag and held it out for me to take. The letter was heavy and bone-coloured, and it was addressed to a young actor I knew that she liked, care of his talent agency, located in that city on the far coast of the other continent. She had written the address on the envelope by hand, in blue ink. 'I want you to post this,' she told me. 'And when you receive the reply, you have to bring it back to me.' I ran the envelope over with my fingertips; we did not use real paper in our classroom very often. It was far better quality and more expensive-looking than any paper I had ever handled.

I handed the envelope back to her, confused. 'If I do post this for you,' I said, 'why would a reply come back to me, when it was you who wrote the letter?' She glanced around the corridor; it was still empty. Some way off, we could make out two guards blocking the large pair of wooden doors that led to the other wings of the building. We could see no minders anywhere nearby. 'Because I put a return envelope inside,' the Queen said, 'with your name and address on it.' Quickly, she reached to tuck the letter into the pocket of my coat. As she did, I caught a brief, clean fragrance. 'My address?' I said. 'How did you get that?' She put her head to one side and folded her arms, and only stared at me.

I knew better than to try to give the letter back a second time. But when I asked her why she could not post it herself, she did what I had begun to recognise she often did when she felt threatened: she switched into an arch, self-aware imitation of one of her minders.

I found this repellent but felt compelled to pretend that I did not, which created in me a queasiness; I often felt this queasiness when I was near her. 'Will you do it, or won't you?' she said, although it was the tone that counted; the same tone her minders used when she was behaving 'unacceptably'. She was used to being pinned by them, and now, copying them, she had pinned me. And I sensed, in any case, that she was frightened.

I took the letter home with me, and when I could, I posted it.

When the reply arrived, delivered care of me at my address just as she had promised, in the same type of envelope as the outgoing letter, only this time with a foreign return postmark, I took it to her as she had asked, taking care to conceal the exchange. She seemed shocked when I passed it over, like she had never expected a reply at all; as if all she had really been expecting in return was trouble. But there had been no trouble. After receiving the post earlier that morning, one of my parents, I did not know which, had simply left the letter for me on the desk in my room, without comment. And now, quite undetected, the Queen slipped it in the pocket of her skirt and took it away with her.

An unfiltered line of communication to and from the outside world: that is what those first two letters gave her for the first time ever, I was almost certain. Whether because of this, or because of the contents of the reply itself (the details of which she did not volunteer, and which I did not ask about), she seemed to light up from the inside in the days that followed. So, again and again, we repeated the procedure. She would write to various of her favourite actors, usually care of their talent management agencies, which were often located on a particular boulevard in that distant city. Then, during shuffles for gym shoes or books, she would leave the letters in my bag for me to post on my journey home. Not always, but mostly, a reply came back. If one did, it would appear one day on my desk in my room without discussion, and I would pass it to her secretly.

Occasionally I wanted to provoke my parents into asking me about the letters. I thought about doing so when my father and I played chess together, or when I was cleaning with my mother before she left for her morning shift, but I never did. I did not want to take the risk. The Queen had begun to side with me against all the others in the class. And sometimes, as we ate our pea soup sitting side by side in the dining room, she would reach underneath the table to take my hand. I imagine that she trusted me.

I never read the Queen's letters, even though I was in possession of them so often, both those she sent out and those she received. I could have, if I'd wanted to. But I never did. She had so little in her life that was her own. And the longer I knew her, the more I understood, or thought I did, how fragile she truly was.

That winter, the false sun of a whole day came and went in class and we did not see her. She had made her mysterious exits and entrances on occasion, but never, prior to this, had she been fully absent; she had always been well physically, never prone to sore throats or flu. That day we heard intermittent shouting, far off in the Palace. The teacher, alert, shut the door. We continued to feel her absence like some sort of wound, all the time aware that in any other, normal school, this would be unheard of, ridiculous. Not for the first time I felt the situation of her life, in its entirety, to be a kind of violence. Sometimes that thought pressed in on me so urgently that I wanted to scream. And yet, I reminded myself, she was my friend. But our friendship, such as it was, felt uneasy; it was too unbalanced to be otherwise.

In refusing the temptation of reading her letters, it was also true that I did not want to violate our bond. Which is to say, I was afraid. I had never expected her to like me, and I had never expected to enjoy it so much that she did. Strangers now occasionally walked up to shake my parents' hands when we were in the supermarket, and our neighbours spoke to us differently when we passed them in the stairwells of our building.

Sometimes the Queen seemed to look at me as if to say, is there nothing more? Her expression burning. As if she expected me to fail her, to fail to keep her secrets. As if she wanted that. I wonder, now, what might have happened if I had obeyed the apparent, unspoken command, rather than the spoken. By then, most of the letters I was sending and receiving on her behalf were addressed to or from one particular well-known actor, a former child star, who was, at that time, aged about seventeen. She had confessed to me, red-faced, the obvious truth that yes, this actor had taken to corresponding with her, but she revealed no more than that. I felt in no position to press her further on it.

The President winked at me when I saw him next, on the day of the parade. Our National Day, which he had moved to midwinter's day by then. Celebrating at midwinter reminded us, the President said, how the country had found its unity and purpose in the depths of greatest loss. That year, I paraded beside her in national costume. In an armoured car. Our two pairs of knees, side by side. I only sat there, while she waved. Beside the car, which crawled along, the soldiers' buttons, shining. And when it stopped: his offered arm for her, and that one, small wink, for me.

I kept that costume a long time, remembering how my parents would watch that evening's broadcast over and over again, as if it was the final proof they had been seeking that they had arrived and were citizens of this country.

One night at the end of winter my father woke me – the Palace had phoned my parents; the Queen had requested me. I would have to dress quickly. My father was already dressed. In the car he rubbed impatiently at the inside of the windscreen with his handkerchief to remove the condensation. We drove the eight or nine miles to the Palace in falling snow. The gates opened for us, and a guard in the gatehouse beckoned my father in. The usual guards were not present. Inside, a minder spoke to me softly and began guiding me upstairs with an arm on my elbow. I looked back and saw another one speaking quietly to my father. On an upper landing I looked down, peering over the balustrade, and saw my father walking back towards the door. Then, through a window on the first floor: his footprints in the fresh snow, his car door closing. I watched him drive away.

We went further into the Palace than I'd ever been before, into a different wing from where our schoolrooms were. It was low-lit and sleek and modern. The minder showed me through to her bedroom. Except for the light from the large television screen, it was completely dark. The television had been muted but blaring across it was a movie. The Queen was in her bed, sunk back on many pillows, wrapped in a quilt covered in raised, red roses. On the far wall, beside the bed, I noticed an irregularly shaped dark patch. The patch was liquid, dripping.

She had not been able to sleep, she said. She had screamed, she said, until she had persuaded them to get me. She was half smiling now. She was proud. Her eyes flashed with the light from the TV. She had taken on that arch manner again; I could see her spine straighten, the lining up of her vertebrae. What she *wanted*, she said, was for me to watch her favourite film with her. She patted the bed, beside her. Now my eyes had adjusted I could see a lamp on the floor, too, beyond the bed, lying horizontally and with glass fragments all around it. It was not lit; it appeared to be entirely broken.

I turned to look for permission, but nobody was there. Someone had silently closed the door behind me. My heart flowered up. I felt, for a moment, like I wanted to run. It was not clear what was expected of me, or even how I was allowed to be with her here, alone. But when I climbed in beside her, the covers were thick and heavy, and my beating chest eased. I sat upright against the pillows, too; there were enough for both of us. The roses on her quilt were each the size of my abdomen. She switched the sound on. The actors had the accent of the other continent, which was not especially familiar to me.

This, this was her favourite, she told me. It was a film in black and white. 'But it's not old,' she said. 'Not as old as you'd think.'

On screen, a girl sat with a man in an old-fashioned car. You saw them front on, as if you were lying on the bonnet. The girl clutched a battered tin box on her lap as the car bumped across a barren landscape. 'It's called *Paper Moon,*' the Queen said. 'He's her father and she's helping him to run his cons. But it turns out that she's better at it than he is. And he doesn't like it very much.'

I said nothing. I watched. The car pulled up in front of a house and the man and the girl climbed out. The man fetched a Bible from the boot of the old-fashioned car and took it with him to knock on the door of the house. The girl in the film wore a hat and had a fixed little face. 'You'll like this,' said the Queen. She paused the film and mimicked the girl's line. '*Give me back my two hundred dolla!*' I had to do it too, she told me, and she laughed until I did. Eventually, we laughed together. '*You trying to keep secrets from me?*' we repeated, over and over, like the woman at the door of the hotel room where the man was trying to keep the girl hidden. '*You got diamonds and rubies in there?*' Once the woman left, the girl sat up in bed and lit a cigarette.

She had her own box underneath her bed. Inside were sweets, and we shared them, and we wondered together what it would be like to smoke a real cigarette. She was happy in my company. She sounded how they always wanted her to sound. I didn't know whether I had underestimated or misunderstood her, this girl beside me in the bed.

She picked at a tiny loose thread on one of the bed-quilt roses, and she chewed on a liquorice lace. And then, 'My grandmother,' she said to me, 'rode her bicycle to school every day. Even when it was snowing.' She nodded towards the Park, which ran to the north of the Palace, towards the centre of the capital, just as it had done in her grandmother's day, and for hundreds of years before. The Park was full of enormous, ancient trees, but its lawns were always mowed and its paths were always busy. You could ride a bike there any time you liked.

I stared at the sweet wrappers strewn across the bed. I did not know what to say. She made me tired. Her contradictions. I wanted to lie down properly then, and I did. She lay down too, and then she put her head on my shoulder. I felt my breath catch in my ribs. I felt like a failure. I felt that there was something I had missed. We might have been lying in a coffin, it was so dark in the room. She smelled of soap and lavender, and I fell asleep, and when I closed my eyes I could see images in black and white from *Paper Moon*.

When I woke, she was no longer beside me; I lay in the bedspread of roses alone. Someone had tidied away the wrappers and lamp and broken glass, and the slick of liquid on the wall, and they had set a glass of juice beside the bed. The curtains were still drawn, and the snow was bright outside when I got up and peeked through them. On her dresser, framed photographs of her horses. On weekends she went into the countryside to ride the horses. That is what the minders told us. I had never heard her talk about them. Was it that she did not want to make us jealous?

I felt a terrible aloneness. My stomach ached. Her room was too precise, it was exhausting and oppressive. I went outside into the corridors, and nobody was there. They were chill and carpeted. They might have gone on forever. I chose a direction and I walked. Finally, as I rounded a corner, a minder was there. She seemed to be anticipating me, folding her hands in front of her as soon as she saw me. She took me to my father, who was already waiting for me in the forecourt, his woollen hat held pathetically in his hands.

B ut it is the second time I was summoned that is important. What I have to tell you concerns, more closely, that second time. My parents were notified in advance. A weekend date was fixed, and at the appointed time a driver came to collect me in one of the Palace cars. Since that night in her room, we had sometimes shared our special jokes together at school. But as the weeks passed and the weather warmed, the Queen came to class on fewer and fewer days. We did not know for certain where she was when she was not in school, but occasionally noises of disturbance would reach us in the schoolrooms, and I pictured her shouting and destroying her possessions. We saw her minders less frequently, and when we did see them they would walk past us with their heads down, apparently preoccupied. The Queen had missed events scheduled at the Palace as well as several broadcasts, and I had been approached in the street by people concerned for her welfare. I had been waiting for her to hand me another letter, but she had not. In the back of the sleek, silent vehicle, I burned with the idea that she wanted to be with me again.

I was driven up to an unfamiliar Palace entrance: a small, nondescript door I had difficulty placing in relation to the other sections of the building. It led into a corridor that was dark and low-ceilinged and smelled of damp. Inside, a minder that I recognised a little greeted me. She stood with her hands clasped together in front of her. She seemed relaxed, but I sensed that this was a performance, a highly contrived effect.

'I do need to thank you for coming,' she said. She inclined her head towards me as she spoke. Her tone suggested we were resuming a conversation we had not had. 'How wonderful for you, to be the Queen's best friend.' I didn't think that was true, I told her. She shook her head at me; I could tell it was very important to her that I understood I was wrong. 'Not at all,' she said. 'You are special to her. That has become very clear to us.'

The minder gestured for me to sit down with her on a nearby chaise. It did not look valuable but was worn; a functional piece of furniture, not decorative. It had been placed near a large door, which was held ajar by a bundle of electrical cables snaking out of the bottom. They flowed out into the corridor in which we were sitting and continued along it, down to my left and out of sight. A man wearing headphones rounded the corner with a jug of water and several tumblers on a tray. He did not glance at me for even a moment before opening the door with the cables and taking the tray inside.

'As you are surely aware,' the minder said, 'the Queen is not currently herself.' I said nothing, feeling as if I must give nothing away. 'This is very sad,' she said. 'We here at the Palace need her to be well. Her country needs her to be well.' I nodded a small agreement; I felt compelled to agree in some part. I briefly felt the fact of my being alone, here, with this woman. Earlier, when they called for me, it had been that rare occasion when my father was out and my mother was at home; she was recovering from a bad flu and had been unable to work. She had greeted the Palace staff with deference and had ushered me out of the door of our flat as quickly as she could manage; my father might, perhaps, have taken the opportunity to enquire in person why again it was that I was requested.

The minder wrapped her linked hands around her crossed knees. 'We are all mindful,' she said, 'of exactly how unusual this situation is.' She let her eyes roam broadly, to indicate our surroundings. 'We empathise very much with the Queen's distress. And it has taken those of us in charge of her care a long time to devise, in consultation with certain world-class experts, what we believe to be an appropriate solution.' Her face was grave. 'I hear you are a very clever child,' she said. 'Am I correct?' Again, I felt I had to nod; a terrible repeat. I felt choreographed. 'I thought so,' she said. She began to smile, and her hand reached out and settled on my knee. 'That's why I have no doubt that you will understand exactly what we need, and why we need it.'

The Queen was, the minder told me, in need of a break. 'A holiday?' I said. 'No,' said the minder. 'We have offered her a holiday, but she will not go. Did you know that she is afraid to leave the Palace? Impossibly afraid?' I frowned at the minder. 'No, that isn't true,' I said. 'On weekends she rides her horses in the countryside.' The minder shook her head. 'Have you ever seen her ride a horse?' she asked. 'Have you ever been there at the time?' I hadn't, I told her, but I was sure I'd seen a picture of it. 'That's right,' she said. 'You've seen a picture.' Apparently, I had pleased her greatly, but I still didn't understand.

She would explain, she said, from the beginning. 'The Queen does not ride horses,' she said, 'but it pleases many people to believe that she does. So, from time to time, we construct a picture of her riding, and then we put that picture on the news sites, where everyone can see it.' But the picture isn't real, I said. 'The picture isn't real,' she repeated, 'but the happiness it brings is real. And all the while, don't forget,' said the minder, 'the Queen has been at home, safe in the Palace like she wanted to be.' I said nothing; I continued to listen. Then, she fixed me very steadily in her gaze. 'Now imagine,' she went on, 'that instead of making picture after picture, we could make a version of the Queen, a kind of copy of her, that we could use in videos, and which could even, in certain special places with certain special equipment, take her place in real life. Then the Queen could always have a rest when she needed to, without anybody being worried about her or becoming cross about it.' She paused, and I knew she was waiting to gauge my response. I swallowed before I spoke. 'Nobody should be cross with her,' I said. 'She isn't even a grown-up yet.' The minder blinked a number of times. 'Well,' she said, 'perhaps that's so. But we cannot change what is.'

She swept me through the rest of it, which she said would all be very simple. The Palace had already hired the best craftsmen and -women in the world to create her copy. But to be able to do it, she said, they needed to capture her reactions. And they needed to be strong ones, authentic ones. Ones that only a close friend, like me, someone she truly cared for, could help to evoke. 'Her reactions?' I asked. 'Yes,' the minder said, 'like laughter, fear, sorrow. We must record them closely. We need to capture her feelings to allow them to exist outside of her.'

I did not know what she meant by this. I kept staring at the minder's dark red lipstick, which did not shine in any way. I wanted some of that water I had seen pass by in the jug on the tray. I was thirsty. There was something dreamlike I couldn't break through, as if I were in a memory. I could barely hear my own voice. The minder sat patiently, observing me.

I asked her what it was, exactly, that they needed me to do.

The minder smiled again. 'Come,' she said. 'She wishes to see you.' Then she stood and showed me through to the room.

The walls were hung with screens of blue fabric and there were no windows, no paintings. Inside the room were five or six people, quiet and dressed in black, behind cameras of various sizes and shapes on tripods and dollies, or holding tall, jointed microphone booms at various angles. At the centre of the room was a table, piled with neatly folded clothes and boxes of various sizes, such as you might find in an expensive store. Beside it the Queen stood waiting for me, her expression placid and unreadable. I could not tell, and knew I would have no opportunity to ask, how she felt about the minders' plan, or even to what extent she knew its details. Was it her plan too, I wondered? Did she know what was going to happen? Her presence, I told myself, seemed to imply that she had agreed, at least in some small part. 'Look,' she said, that same flat expression in her eyes. 'We're allowed to play.'

A soft-spoken word: the cameras began to roll. She pulled at something knitted and pink, which sprang loose, gutting itself readily. A sweater. She slipped it over her head. I did not know how to play with clothes. They were dumb under my fingers. I passed her, shyly, a pair of neat-heeled shoes. She put them on with quick, demure motions of her ankles. At the edges of the room, the silent, black figures.

On the table there was jewellery too, and I asked if it was real. She said she supposed some was; she didn't herself know which of the pieces here were real, and which were not. Every item in her collection, she told me, had a companion version, an imitation almost impossible to distinguish from the genuine. It was safer that way, she said. She was happy now, and began to perform for the cameras. She placed a necklace on my collarbone, but I shucked it off; it felt alien and heavy. She took off her beaded bracelet and replaced it with one that looked as if it was made of diamonds and rubies. Everything sparkled and glowed underneath the spotlights.

After a time, minders brought seats up to the table, and then, while we sat, it was cleared and then re-piled, this time with food. The Queen took the diamond bracelet off and put her beaded one back on. We could hear murmurs: instructions, directions perhaps. In the peripheries, the cameras and microphones shifted positions. We forgot about them for a while. We began to eat, and to laugh. How could we not? We were giggling and stuffing our mouths with pastry when the clown came. He had a harlequin costume and a heavily painted face, and he came and stood beside us on a little plinth. He gave the Queen a bunch of paper flowers. She and I looked at one another, uncertain if this was a joke. With a raise of my eyebrows, and her almost imperceptible shrug in return, we agreed that we would play along. The clown juggled and made balloon animals and acted out little slapstick scenes with them before offering them to us.

For a time I forgot where I was and what I was doing. It felt good to be like a child. To have treats offered you, to delight in them, to share them with another. This, then, was happiness. I felt pleased to know, finally, what it was. But only a moment later, I saw her face seize. She was staring at the clown. She had become rigid. When I looked, I saw it for myself. The clown's smile had creased his caked white make-up, revealing something of his brows, and of the trenches running downwards from his nose. They were familiar. Once you noticed that, then you could see it, too, in the way he moved his arms. Could it be true? That the clown in the harlequin costume was, in fact, the President?

The Queen's eyes fell to her plate, and her back straightened even further. She began to tremble. I set my own plate down. The cameras shifted collectively, and creaked as they did. The peak of happiness had passed. You could feel it. Her hair had fallen over her face. The clown took off his hat and bowed, and then retreated.

Movement at the edges of the room, among the black-clad figures. A minder went to the Queen, patting my arm in light acknowledgement as she passed. 'Well done, my dear,' she said to her. I had never heard any of them call her that before, or any appellation like it. The minder pushed the Queen's hair behind her ears and ran her fingers down the Queen's cheekbone, then her jaw. I could see now that the Queen was crying. 'Quickly,' said the minder. She announced this to the room. 'Quickly now,' she said.

One of the figures in black pulled a projection screen down from the ceiling, so large it covered the whole wall in front of us, as if we were in a cinema. The microphone booms and cameras adjusted their positions. The minder squeezed the Queen's shoulders and then she moved back to stand by the wall. The Queen was frightened, I could tell. Quiet again, and stillness. Behind us, a projector hummed and lit the screen. What would I have said to her, then, if I could have? It is impossible to know. I wanted time to breathe, but there was none. I was frightened, too. I had guessed what was coming.

My parents had been careful to prevent me from seeing the footage, wrapping their hands around my eyes or ushering me quickly out of rooms when necessary. We had, ourselves, fled violence, albeit of a different kind, though I remembered nothing of that. I knew only facts: that the footage was one minute and four seconds long; that, though always called 'the footage', it had, in fact, been compiled from video taken by two drones, both positioned near the church the Royal Family were entering that morning. I knew that she had been held by her mother for most of the film's duration, and for a short time afterwards by her uncle. Those were the technical details on which I tried to focus. But of course, they meant nothing. In particular, I had anticipated nothing of the sounds. They seemed to come at me from all directions, even from inside. It was in my belly that I felt the hot staccato of the automatic weapon; in my own throat that the voices curdled into panic.

Observing her, I knew that she had never seen the footage, either. She kept her eyes open throughout. She did not collapse, not even once the projector was turned off and silence returned, raw and overwhelming. Yet, the sadness which had overcome her was thorough and real. The capturing process had surely been successful, her responses now available for use. I could not help but admire her. I realised I had never seen her stronger. Other, perhaps, than in the final moments of the video, in which she alone, miraculously unharmed, stands and reaches out her tiny arms.

During those final moments, did I reach across to hold her hand? I am sorry to say that I did not. My chair was not positioned close enough to hers, and it had not felt appropriate to move it. The room was warm but I felt held in place by ice. Had the positioning of the chair been purposeful, I wondered? Had I been supposed to comfort her? Or had I done as they intended? Had I failed, or succeeded?

After that, they took her away. She was ushered behind the curtain of blue fabric. The food and the clown's gifts were cleared from the table. I was offered water, and as I drank I spilled it on myself, as if I had forgotten the proper usage of my mouth.

It was suggested I stroll the parterre, and, for an hour or so, I did. It was late afternoon by then. The breeze in the gardens was fresh and full of the sea. I tried very hard to think of nothing at all and felt queasy whenever I failed. So much blood, blooming into all those colourful clothes. I did not want to take the path that would return me to the small, nondescript door. I did not want to go back inside that room. In the centre of each of the parterre beds lavender flowered, and to make myself feel better I rubbed a head or two between my fingers and breathed it in.

I had reached one edge of the garden and was doubling back to begin another lap when I saw the President approach. He wore his usual rolled sleeves, and as he grew nearer I repeatedly glanced at his face, but I could see not a single trace of make-up there nor any tinge of white. He was inscrutable. I knew that I would never know, could never know, whether it had been he in the harlequin costume or whether she and I together had imagined it.

He put his hand between my shoulder blades. He turned on his heels, executing a move; we were walking back to the Palace now, together. I felt strangely limp underneath his touch. 'You have done very well,' he told me. 'And there is only one more thing we require you to do.' I stopped and turned to face him. He regarded me with what I felt was pleasure. 'This time,' he said, 'you need to make her angry.' The breeze blew around the two of us. 'She is angry all the time,' I said. I was afraid I had spoken out of turn, but he laughed and patted my back more firmly. 'That is anger to which she is accustomed,' he said. 'With you, it will be real and new. We want you to play chess with her and cheat.' He winked at me again, like on the day of the parade. 'She doesn't like to lose, you know. She isn't good at second-best.'

At the end of the path ahead, a minder saw us approach and held open the door. I stopped walking again. The warm breeze came up once more as the President fixed on me, and I smelled the lavender and the ocean both, beneath the top note of his cologne. I had, perhaps, not ever felt as much alone. 'I don't want to do that,' I said. He sighed, then, a small, brisk noise, and took his hand from my back. 'There will be many times in your life when you won't want to do what you must,' he told me. 'When you are older, you will remember this as the first time. Have you not enjoyed living here in this country? Have we not made you safe and welcome?' Yes, I told him, of course. 'And don't you think that you should do your duty, just as she does?' I felt helpless. My stomach pulled on me. Eventually, I said that I could, yes. I told him that I would.

Inside the blue-screened room the Queen was sitting at the table again, the chessboard set before her. She seemed refreshed, renewed. Her hair had been dampened and swept back, and her lips seemed to have regained some of their colour. She wore a simple navy dress, one I had not seen before. Her skinny knees were bumping up and down. 'Let's play?' she said. I glanced behind me; the President nodded, almost invisibly, and slipped among the dark figures standing by the wall. I sat down, and the room became silent. The cameras once again began to roll.

The board was set to a standard opening, a chess problem of a kind I often set up at night on my small magnetic set. Before I went to sleep, I would think my way into the problem, in the hopes that when I woke, I would know the best solution. More often than not, this is what happened. Now, I was supposed to cheat. She was still pistoning her feet. For a moment I imagined her skin to be transparent so that I could see the tendons working underneath.

We played a few moves without speaking. For the first time, I saw her glance occasionally towards the figures at the edges of the room, and at the cameras and booms in operation; prior to now, she had seemed intent on maintaining the fiction that they were not present. Surely, this task I had been set was nonsense, a joke.

Did she know what my objective in our game was going to be? Did she know the intended outcome was her fury? Surely, I thought, that could not be true. My task would be impossible if it was. And if it wasn't, what *was* she expecting? She seemed to be expecting something.

I wanted so desperately to ask her, but I could not. There was a weight of expectation in the room that was palpable, and which I greatly feared to disappoint. I did not know how to disobey, but I realised, hopelessly, that I could not cheat, either. My thinking felt smudged over; my fingers simply would not make the moves. I could take my fists and sweep the pieces off the board, but I suspected this would delight her, rather than anger her.

I lifted my rook, and then I set it down again. I took a breath, and for a moment, I shut my eyes. Desperate this time, undaunted, I shuffled my chair closer. Then, I leaned to whisper in her ear. At the edge of my vision I noticed the cameras and sound booms moving in response, the better to capture her. I covered my lips with my hand. 'I told the minders about your letters,' I said. 'I gave them every reply to read before I even passed them to you. They sealed them back up afterwards, so you couldn't tell.' My nose pressed close to her hair, my chin to her neck; she smelled, again, of lavender. She was poised, trembling. I could feel how rigid she was. 'I showed some of the others in the class too,' I said. 'We all kept it secret. We laughed about the letters every day on our way home.'

I sat back, and I saw her blue eyes seem to flatten against the screen walls, and her shaking began to gather its own momentum. It was like a video we had watched once in class, of a bridge across a distant peninsula set to vibrating so violently by the wind one day that it collapsed. When she picked up the solid wooden board, the pieces fell away to the ground like the bridge parts falling into the water. She held the board horizontal when she hit me with it.

When I was able to sit up, a car took me home. It was nearly dark by then. My mother had made a stew and my father was ironing. They smiled at me and said nothing, refusing to violate their shared wall of silence, which surrounded the details of my life inside the Palace. For many days I was worried that the ringing in my ear might be permanent.

L ess than a month later, I saw it for the first time. I was watching the evening broadcast with my father. An artist had come to teach us how to paint in a pointillist style and was explaining how the dots were like pixels on a screen. The Queen and I were shown painting side by side, though she had not been present that day. She was ill, a minder had told us. She needed to rest. An easel had been set up for her in the art room, and nobody had used it. But in the broadcast, there she was: painting. Her bright eyes, flicking up and down from her work; her curling hair, backlit by the window. I looked over at my father. He was delighted every time he saw me in a broadcast.

It was the first of many. Her absences grew in length and number. And in the evenings, she appeared on the screen in places I knew for certain she had not been: climbing a rope ladder in the ballroom; tending to tomato seedlings in the greenhouse; baking cookies. At school, the faces of the other children were impenetrable. I tried to make friends but it was as if I was diseased. On those occasions when she was in class with us, the Queen looked at me as if I were not a real person; as if I were dead. She had fallen so far behind in her schoolwork that the teachers had stopped even making her try to do the same as everyone else. I watched her closely to see if she had found another friend, but she had not. She did not respond to the kind words of the long-plaited girl any more than she did mine. I wanted to ask her: what is it you do when you're not in class? Where do you go? Do you only watch films and television? But she would not speak to me at all. Occasionally, as we all shuffled into the dining room for lunch or jostled in the corridor putting on our coats, I reached out to touch her with my fingers, so lightly that she did not notice, to check that she was still real. I was always reassured that she was. But still, I ached, because I had lost her anyway.

I n the summer I received notice that my place in the class had been terminated. My mother received a transfer to a position in the north and I began attending a new school. At first, because I was recognised from the broadcasts, we were a little famous, and people kept their distance. But this celebrity did not persist; after two or three years it was all but forgotten, and we were like anyone else in that small town, which lay under snow for most months of the year. The broadcasts were different by then. They had already taken on a form very close to what is familiar today: a casual address on a matter of interest, highlighting commendable acts, perhaps, or relating an inspirational story, five to seven minutes in duration, the Queen speaking in a warm and reassuring manner to the camera, in one of her rooms, sometimes in conversation with the President. And twice a year, an appearance on the balcony, or, at least, an appearance at which she could be seen through it, since she always remained standing within the balcony's open French doors, just inside the Palace itself. Never in person, or even in close proximity. Never shaking hands. The Queen had been diagnosed with an immune illness, they said. She was now individually schooled.

On several occasions, I tried to contact her. But my letters were returned unopened. To wait near the Palace itself in hope of a glimpse, as many people did, was fruitless, impossible. Her seclusion was rigid and absolute. Or so you were supposed to assume. Such was the illusion, the mechanics of the lie. I knew nobody who doubted that the monarch they saw daily on their screens was real. It was possible that, since I had known her personally once, they simply did not voice their doubts in front of me. But I did not think so. After all, the Queen offers daily comfort, and over time I had come to accept that belief in her provides its own reward. ■

HÖLZUNG

Muhammad Salah

Introduction by Esther Kinsky

To begin with – a sequence of photographs. Pictures which to every beholder will ring a different set of distant bells. Light, colours, landscape, faces – they all trigger memories, and memories make connections, each of them differently. I prefer my gaze to be unencumbered by expectation or knowledge. Free to find its own little hook to latch on to, the fragment to engage with, the resurfacing memory to abandon itself to. But what is an unencumbered gaze? And where does it begin to see?

I see a road, a dual carriageway, yellow street signs, a few cars. A road of departure, arrival, passage. A road that could be anywhere – anywhere in Germany. Having grown up in Germany, I'm inevitably reminded of similar roads lined by woodland in the bleak season, without a view ahead. Through the photographer's eye I see the road from above. Perhaps from a footbridge, linking woodland and woodland. An unsteady structure, swaying under gusts of wind, shaking when a heavy lorry passes underneath. The surface is coarse, creaking and trembling underfoot. I grew up in a land of shuddering footbridges spanning expressways, and I remember the thud of feet on those bridges, running. I remember the flat yellow of road signs like the one on the picture, and a river, a floodplain, rows of poplars, the fringes of a town. Walls of rough concrete marked by time and weather, steel railings colder than ice, and fires in early winter when the dead leaves were burned.

I'd like to be a blank surface for the pictures to impress themselves on. But unlike recalling, forgetting is not a question of effort. The remembered thud of feet running on a footbridge in my childhood comes up against a name I couldn't help taking in: *Khartoum*.

Here, in this land of footbridges, woodland and concrete walls, the daylight is vague and grey; it blurs edges and brings out the solitude of a red window frame and the helplessness of purple creeper foliage while the leafless crowns of trees melt into the vagueness. It's a light that sits oddly next to the sound of *Khartoum*, which I imagine to be infused with hues of yellow, orange and red, perhaps a little hazy with desert dust.

The light around the woodland is familiar to me, it instantly brings back memories of childhood winters. Whether I like it or not, they're there, emerging unbidden along with words like 'clammy' and 'black ice'. But there's something to be said for this light too: it's an even light, muted and shadowless; it lets things come into their own in a quiet way. No weighing of sharp contrasts between light and dark, no assessment of shadows. Even the coarse concrete seems less stark than it would in the sunshine; it looks porous, as if a soft crackle ran through the texture every now and then, the wintery sighs of lifeless matter. This light without shadows may become a photographer's friend, regardless of the cold and in spite of its foreignness in the face of the name *Khartoum*.

The muted light seeps through the windows into rooms that speak of a life led around desk, clutter, house plants and bed. It spreads over the objects, smooth surfaces and the textures of fabrics; it finds itself reflected in the wooden floor, and, however feeble, it manages to infuse the cloth hanging above the bed, the curtain and the fingery leaves of the house plant, with warmth and colour. It encourages an exchange between the patches in orange and yellow within and the little shreds of autumnal red on branches outside the window, a low-key chatter, familial.

My gaze is moving back and forth between the pictures, trying to find links and threads between objects and views. Is there a conversation among the colours, the warm and the cold ones trying to find common ground? A common language? I'm wondering if the spaces framed by the lens – outside, inside, cold space, warm space – are in a city, a town, a village? No clues. Do the spaces relate to the woman who appears in three of the photographs, the obvious you to the I and eye behind the lens? Once, she's a haloed figure, wrapped up in winter clothes. Then she's inside, arms crossed, shoulders tense, her face unsheltered. Is she cold? Defiant? Angry? Sad? The space around her is contracting. Next there's a close-up of the back of her head with hardly any space left between the lens and herself. This view of her short hair, her ear, her cheekbone, blurred and pale, adds a colour of tenderness to the sequence. And some melancholy too. And what about herself? This time she won't meet the gaze of the lens. Is her head bent over a book? Writing? Shards? No clues.

The reds and yellows in the pictures guide the gaze. Yellow is the cloth on the wall that seems to say: home. Orange is the colour that defies the cold. There are the leaves of the house plant, the poster on the wall. The halo of the wrapped-up figure in the night. Copper is the colour of the woman's hair in the close-up. Points of reference that hold their own against the grey light and the cold. But silence hangs in the air. I imagine words curling on the speakers' lips and falling to the ground with a dull little clack. Someone will have to sweep them up at some point.

There's a second place name I've learned by now, besides *Khartoum*: *Marienhölzung*. *Hölzung* is a beautiful, ancient word, denoting a small area of woodland, a copse. It's a rare word, endangered like some birds and butterflies. *Marienhölzung* means: Marie's woodland. I know that the photographer's name is Muhammad. And what about the woman? She too wants a name, a name for her wrapped-up figure in the night, for her face, for the back of her head, her short hair, her cheekbone and ear. I'd call her Marie.

That would make the pictures of her *Marienbilder* in German, pictures of Marie, not to be confused with images of the Virgin Mary, regardless of her halo in the winter night outside. Muhammad the photographer is looking at Marie, he's probing her image, exploring spaces around Marie and her Hölzung; he a stranger to this grey light, she wary, hesitant, perhaps, to let him partake of her winter.

D o the pictures want to tell a tale, say, of an arrival, an encounter, of the winter cold and a void? Or is it only my gaze that wants to read this tale, or at least an account of varying degrees of closeness and of separation? Every lens frames the world, and for a while we as beholders look and name and draw or jump to conclusions as if the frame were the world. My eye wanders from one rectangular view of a life to the next – no, it's two lives: one of the seeing and one of the seen, and both remain a mystery. As so often when I look at the faces of people on photographs I'm briefly stunned by the thought that I as the beholder, a nameless nobody outside Marie's life, will never know what her gaze, so deceptively directed at me, perceives.

That's perhaps where a story could set in, a story that would be determined as much by my sense of cold and warm and light and colour and space as by the photographer's choice of frame. The story would be brief but inevitable, arising from the deeply human desire to connect the dots on a mental map. A map which unfolds whenever memories have been stirred from their sleep by a particular light, colour, or sound. Memories want to speak.

And – speaking of maps – how does the final picture wrap up the sequence? This close-up of an old map, apparently of a part of *Marienhölzung*, Marie's woodland. Vaguely reminiscent of a map for a treasure hunt in a children's book, it shows the course of a brook, dashed patches for moors and a prominent *Brandplatz*. Another ancient-sounding name. *Brandplatz* indicates a place for burning. Is it this map Marie is looking at while the lens and the eye behind it dwell on the back of her head, her ear and her cheekbone? Is she looking for clues – to find a treasure or to bury one, or for a place to light a fire, a wild flush of orange in the muted light of winter, to consume mementoes, to cut through the clamminess, to distract from the thud of feet running on the footbridge?

The tale takes us to a place for burning, but not to an ending. It takes us to a map, and maps are always about beginnings. ∎

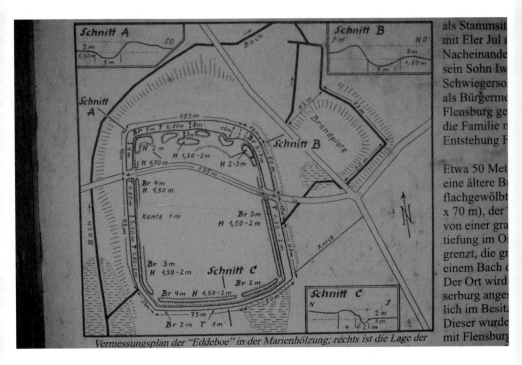

Vermessungsplan der "Eddeboe" in der Marienhölzung; rechts ist die Lage der

als Stammsit
mit Eler Jul
Nacheinande
sein Sohn Iw
Schwiegerso
als Bürgerm
Flensburg ge
die Familie n
Entstehung F

Etwa 50 Met
eine ältere B
flachgewölbt
x 70 m), der
von einer gra
tiefung im O
grenzt, die gr
einem Bach
Der Ort wird
serburg anges
lich im Besitz
Dieser wurde
mit Flensburg

AN ENGLISH OPENING

Maxim Osipov

TRANSLATED FROM THE RUSSIAN
BY ALEX FLEMING

The autumn years, their very beginning – seventy, seventy-five, life goes on. Many of the participants in this year's tournament will live another fifteen, even twenty years, though of course these aren't their salad days: everything is already determined, realized. Still, they are the lucky ones: men of means, they get by without outside help – a comfortable life, secure. At some point the decisive loss will come: every life must end in defeat (or, more bluntly, must end) – but that much is fair, necessary even, no? Routine, in any case. Death is not discussed in their circles.

But in the meantime, why not get the gang together, move some pieces around a board? After much writing and wrangling, they had pooled together some funds for an annual tournament. '96 – Philadelphia, '97 – Providence, '98 – little Williamstown, northwestern Massachusetts: frankly, none of the shabbiest corners of their *star-spangled* land for a gathering of aging chess-lovers. This year it was San Francisco's turn. One of the players arranged it all, from the accommodation to the venue. On their rest day they all went out to the Symphony Hall together, took a drive around the town.

The games were played at the Marines' Memorial Club, the players their own spectators, arbiters and organizers, too. Of course, the odd veteran would also stop by for a look – Second World War, Korea,

Vietnam: over the past century their homeland had had its fair share of wars. A great, powerful nation. Two rows of tables, sixteen players, everyone plays everyone, three rounds then a rest day. In previous years there had been as many as twenty players; some fall by the wayside, but others appear, just pay your entry and *welcome to the club.*

The muffled tap of pieces, soft lighting, the occasional quiet remark (chatter at the table is frowned upon); the smells of coffee and polished floors. Smoking is prohibited, of course, but no one smokes as it is – these men aren't enemies unto themselves. In the evenings they fill in the chart together, determine the day's most beautiful game, analyze it. The pleasant, understated world of chess.

B ut everything must come to an end, including the tournament, and its players fly their separate ways: north to Seattle, south to San Diego, to the East Coast. They part ways warmly, though this year's tournament proved rather . . . unusual, shall we say.

The flight for New York leaves with a slight delay. Coach is around 70 percent full, while in first class there are only two passengers, both ours, from our tournament: Albert A. Alexander, former ambassador to Norway (the title sticks for life), and Donald, a businessman, *call me Don.*

Albert is wearing light chinos, a pink button-down shirt and a dark blue, single-breasted blazer. A diplomatic bearing, the image of a peacemaker, he is elegant, handsome, even. Though admired and loved as a man, as a chess player he is decidedly average.

Don's life – or the first seventy-five and a half years of it, he jokes – was devoted to quite different pursuits: selling ball bearings. We Anglo-Saxons love to make light of things, play ourselves down: in actual fact Don was king of the market, scourge of his rivals, with factories in Malaysia, South America and other far-flung places besides. Pensioners in his position have a tendency to strut around the citadels of European civilizations in long shorts and baseball caps, visor flipped backwards for others' amusement; clowns. Beefy Don is no such man. In addition to being one of the best players in the tournament, he is also its longstanding treasurer. And though his weight may be substantial, he runs every morning.

So what do these two men talk about? It is clear just by looking at them that on many matters (prayer in schools, single-sex marriage, gun control, what else? Oh, abortion, capital punishment, healthcare reforms . . .) their opinions will diverge. As Churchill put it: *Democracy is the worst form of government, except for all those other forms that have been tried from time to time.* Both men are acutely aware of this paradox, the diplomat especially so. But what is important is that Albert and Don have both served their families and their nation well.

This year's tournament, however, had been pretty dispiriting for everyone involved. Two talking points – A and I – where to begin? A: Alzheimer's. Poor old Jeremy Levine, all-around nice guy and keeper of traditions, was in a terrible state. At least he could still remember how the pieces move, thank God. His openings were instinctive, confident, but after that it would all fall apart. His opponents, eyes averted, would propose a draw at the first opportunity. Ten, fifteen moves, and then – *Jeremy, what do you say?*

Jeremy had always been an affable man, but at the tournament he had developed a constant giggle – a shy, quiet titter. Honestly, it was uncomfortable being around him, a gray-haired child. Yes, he still recognizes some people, but everyone knows that that, too, will end, the only question is when. The progression of Alzheimer's is impossible to predict.

'He did recognize me,' the ambassador declares.

Don isn't moved by such things:

'That's beside the point.'

What Don had found most galling wasn't so much Jeremy's presence – illness happens, what can you do? – as that of Carolyn, Jeremy's wife: chess is no infirmary. And there had been rather a lot of this Carolyn around, with all her *honey*s and *sweetheart*s. She was at Jeremy's side relentlessly, from chess tables to diaper changes.

'Her whole life she's zipped the man around like a radio-controlled car. Ironic, when she can't even use a computer! Just think, Al – I have to send her letters by snail mail.'

Carolyn believes that reimmersing her husband in chess will slow his decline. According to her, Jeremy was almost back to where he had been a year before.

'The great fruits of our labor,' Don chuckles. 'Makes the whole long flight worthwhile.'

Their meal arrives. The conversation moves on.

'But seriously, if you have no legs then don't expect to ski,' Don says. 'I'm opposed to all those cripple Olympics.'

'You can say that to me, Don, but I wouldn't risk advertising those opinions to a wider audience.'

In any case, it would be inhuman to exclude their old pal from the tournament. And besides – here the ambassador flicks his hand – what's interesting is the process, not the result.

No shit, thinks Don, with the form you've had lately . . .

'Don, you did give Jeremy a draw, didn't you?'

He did. In spite of his convictions.

In-flight conversations have their own stop–start logic. After the meal the old gents feel drowsy.

Would the ambassador mind if Don took a nap? After that they can hash over Ivy, the Russian: a serious matter, something has to be done. Don will shut his eyes, lower his blind for a while, have some time to himself. There, internally, he will see pieces moving across a chessboard, capturing one another, clocks ticking. One winner, one loser: in the world Don wants to live in, all is fair.

The ambassador dozes, too. Below the plane lies America: land of opportunity, leader of the Western world – its tuning fork, if you will. Soon, the ambassador knows, other countries will start to catch up with her, and though that European charm that he holds so dear will inevitably become a thing of the past, life on this planet will become the better, the more humane, for it. Their tournament is a model of rational self-organization, more so than any political party, any social movement: such pure, conflict-free, from-the-heart undertakings are a rarity in today's world. The ambassador has seen a great many difficult, unpleasant things in his time. An awful lot of politics. His knowledge came at a cost.

If anything, the service in first class is excessive. The gentlemen are offered dessert, chocolate mousse. None for Don, thanks. Mousse? What's mousse? Is it like jello? Don hates jello, he can't stand anything that quivers.

'That's gotten me into trouble with the ladies before, believe me,' Don chuckles.

Funny, yes. The ambassador, meanwhile, has loved one woman all his life: his wife. The same goes for Don, of course. But back in their college days . . . Oh, in college we were all polygamous.

The flight is bumpy, not conducive to sleep. The fasten seatbelt sign appears. There is a large river beneath them.

'Just the Missouri or something,' the ambassador suggests.

'Not *just* Missouri,' Don grumbles, who lived in the Midwest for many years.

The ambassador raises his palms – elegantly, like almost everything he does. The Midwest is Don's fiefdom; the ambassador, meanwhile, has only ever lived on the East Coast – in Washington, New York.

S o, how about that Russian? Matthew Ivanov, Ivy. Or as Carolyn, poor old Jeremy's wife, had taken to calling him, *Poison Ivy*.

'Been stung by the poison ivy yet?' she had asked every player.

Yes, they had all been stung, every last one of them. Matthew Ivanov, new kid on the block, had won the entire tournament: fifteen matches, fourteen victories, one draw. And no, the issue here isn't the prize pot – which the winner took outright – but the Russian's attitude to the game, to his competitors.

No one had been able to speak to Matthew, beyond the bare minimum required of the game: before each match – a handshake and *hi*, and then at the end – *that's it, I resign*. Matthew would nod, shake hands and then leave. He never took part in the post-game analyses, not to mention the excursions. And at last night's dinner he had taken his check and framed certificate and ducked out with no more than a *thanks everyone*. Where's that certificate now? Lying in a trash can, for all we know.

'Al, tell me, do you think he even likes chess?'

'The game certainly likes him, Don – more than you or me. Did you see our match?'

No, Don didn't see it.

Albert sighs: when playing a stronger opponent, it forces you to raise your game. But in the ambassador's head-to-head with Ivy, his hands were tied as early as the ninth or tenth move. In a bad position, any move is worthless.

'Where did the kid even come from?' Don wonders.

The ambassador shrugs.

'An immigrant. They like it here.'

'Sure they do – we keep them fed.' Don is annoyed. 'America, the freest country in the world. Too free, if you ask me.'

'There are free countries in Europe, too,' the ambassador says, with a conciliatory tone. He flashes one of his best smiles – the one reserved for his cohorts, allies.

Don has never been to Europe. The ambassador finds this strange.

'You recommend it? What's the point?'

What can you say to that? There are wonderful places.

'But how about you, Don? How long did you hold out against Ivy?'

First off, it was the first game of the tournament. Second, Ivy was playing white. And third, the newbie spent twenty minutes on his opener.

'So the clock's ticking, and I've got this kid I don't know just sitting there in front of me, thinking. His head's down, I can't see his eyes. I mean, what is that, some kind of joke?'

'I imagine he was being entirely serious. He was probably tuning in to his thoughts, deciding whether he was in the mood to play aggressively or beat you in a positional battle. Ivy's a master.'

In the end the youngster had gone with c4, the English Opening. Don responded with e5.

'The Reversed Dragon?' the ambassador asks in delight.

Don nods. It all went by the book. He quickly dictates the moves.

'Know the system?'

'Oh yes, of course,' the ambassador nods.

Like hell he does. Back when Don was running his factories, his ability to tell when he was being lied to saved him from many a sticky situation. He is getting increasingly worked up:

'Look, I can take a kicking, but at least give me something to show for it! But no, he just bleeds you dry, squeezes you like a machine! I'm seventy-five – I can't compute like him! *A master*! I can see he made an impression on you . . .'

'Yes . . .' the ambassador says, as though searching for the right word, one clearly long-since found. 'You know, he has a certain . . .' He is planning on saying 'audacity', but Don interrupts:

'Just say it straight: kid's a hustler. I checked, and there's no chess player by the name of Matthew Ivanov.'

'Don, their alphabet is different. Remember those old sports kits, CCCP?'

'Well I'm telling you, that CCCP of yours was in it for the money!'

'Money? What would he want money for?'

'Al, what does anybody want money for?'

Is this guy out of his mind? Don thinks. Like Jeremy?

Well, if it's the money they're after, the ambassador muses to himself, then why did they sell their politics so cheap?

'Russians have suffered a great deal this century,' the ambassador says contemplatively.

'So you're telling me *the kid* suffered?'

The ambassador continues:

'Perhaps I shouldn't be telling you this, but a few years ago the Russians sold their foreign policy for one million – yes, one *million* – times less than what we were willing to pay them for it.'

They both sit in stunned silence. Don – at the size of the sum, *jeez, one mil, that's six zeros, what kind of money were we sitting on?* The diplomat – at having blabbed to Don.

'I understand,' says the ambassador, breaking the silence. 'We have to protect the spirit of the tournament. How about abolishing the prize fund?'

'We're not an infirmary, Albert. We're not against good players, God no. We just want them to behave properly.'

'So,' the ambassador sighs, 'that means drawing up a code, some rules and regulations. And doing away with winner takes all' – he mimes a staircase with his hand – 'but instead eight thousand, five, three. First, second, third.'

'Yup, it has to be done,' Don nods. 'Because you can bet on it, next time we'll have three of those . . . Ivanovs showing up on our doorstep. Your beloved CCCPs.'

Don is right, of course: their tournament, their great project, their brainchild, is under threat. All this having to lay down the law . . . it's everywhere nowadays, even in family life. Meanwhile, he and Don have done just fine with their old ladies without any such written binders. The four of them should meet up in New York sometime, go to Carnegie Hall or Yankee Stadium . . . then have them over, show them the collection. The ambassador collects owls – marble, clay. He even has a couple of magnificent taxidermies. The owl is a symbol of wisdom.

'The Don, that's a beloved river in Russia. Perhaps that'll redeem them somewhat in your eyes? *And Quiet Flows the Don?*' he says with relish. 'It's a book, it won the Nobel Prize. Not that you, Don, could ever be called quiet.' The ambassador looks out the window, squinting. What is he hoping to find out there?

A t this point there is a minor disturbance. Behind them – where the first-class restroom is – they hear a noise. A young man has quickly slipped inside and locked the door. The stewardess gives the passengers a guilty look, shrugs: *what can you do?* The other restrooms are occupied, someone has clearly had an urgent call of nature and burst into first class.

Soon – too soon, somehow – the sound of the flush is heard, and the young man steps out of the restroom: none other than Matthew Ivanov himself. On recognizing his recent competitors, the young man smiles. His teeth are a brilliant white, but the smile still comes out tense, sad.

Both Don and the ambassador make some bewildered movements, meanwhile Ivanov, who had almost recoiled when he first saw them, now takes a seat in the second row from the back, diagonally behind them. It is clear he hadn't wanted to run into the old men, but that running away from them would have also felt wrong. The only one who can muster a welcoming gesture is the ambassador – not Don, and certainly not the stewardess, who had been on her way to shoo the uninvited guest back into coach, but hesitated on seeing that her wards clearly knew him. The young man, if he did show any aggression, initially showed it only to her.

He pre-empts her: is there really any reason why he can't enjoy a wide, comfy seat for a while? Because his ticket is for economy, the stewardess says. And? Is he disturbing anyone? Is he depriving the others of even a fraction of the comfort they have procured? Still, the stewardess says, it's unfair, wrong. Unfair to the others in economy, and especially unfair to those who have bought first-class tickets. Unfair and immoral.

'Immoral?'

What does this young man find so funny?

'Mr Alexander,' he says, addressing the ambassador, 'do you also feel this way?'

The ambassador shrugs ambiguously.

'I get it, we're not supposed to, but *immoral*?' The young man is inspired: 'Whatever happened to the parable of the vineyard workers: *Is thine eye evil, because I am good?* – know that one, Mr Ambassador?'

Don – who has been strangely quiet so far – strikes his fist onto his table:

'You heard the lady. It's unfair and wrong.' He is red and angry now, like he used to get back when he sold ball bearings.

The young man stands up. The ambassador says, stiffly:

'We respect your aptitude for the game, Matthew, and we should be happy to continue our acquaintance. However, as you can see, this is neither the time nor the place.' He tries to smile nonetheless. 'How I wish I knew Russian like you do English! You had excellent teachers.'

The young man replies:

'Yes, outstanding. And the textbooks were first-rate. As I recall: *What is that noise in the room next door? It is my grandfather eating cheese.*'

Albert, experienced diplomat that he is, knows how to take a blow. He's thinking up a witty retort, but none is needed – the young man is already gone.

After the guest's departure, the old-timers try to piece together the conversation he ruptured.

Don asks:

'What fable was that – about wine?'

'A parable. From Matthew, I think. Yes, very on the nose! My goodness.'

This latest incident has left them both thoroughly shaken. They're elderly men, after all.

'How did you come to know the Scripture so well, Albert?'

'Diplomacy,' the ambassador replies. 'Like it or not, it makes a demagogue out of you.' His charm is gradually returning.

The plane starts to make its descent. Soon after, the Statue of Liberty appears through the windows, a formidable woman holding a book and a torch. The seats are returned to their upright position.

'God knows who we're feeding,' Don ponders, looking at the statue over his neighbor's shoulder.

The ambassador, too, is gazing at the giant sculpture: this lady needs no one; no part of her quivers.

Don asks:

'And you, Albert, what religion do you practice?'

The diplomat replies, a sudden sadness in his voice:

'I don't believe in God.' Then, inexplicably: '*Sir.*' ∎

WATER SPRITES

THE KINGDOM OF SAND

Andrew Holleran

O f the four roads leading out of this town only one looks the way it did forty years ago – and even that, the road to Florahome, is starting to show the small, unmistakable signs that it will end up the way the others have: the forest cut down to build a public storage facility, a Family Dollar, a gas station, a minimart, a housing development. Though the place my father retired to in 1961 is what the real estate agents like to call 'centrally located', that means you must drive about an hour to get anywhere. An hour to the north-east is Jacksonville; two hours to the south is Orlando; thirty minutes to the west is Gainesville; an hour to the east is St Augustine. What lies between these points is a web of small towns, located on average about seven miles from one another: Hawthorne, Lamont, Simmons, Interlachen, Florahome, Carrabelle, Madison, Lawtey, Macclenny, Grandin and Brooker.

'Is it lazy – or does it just look lazy?' a friend from Boston asked years ago when she stopped to have lunch on her drive south. 'Both,' I said. One of the great appeals of Florida has always been the sense that the minute you get here you have permission to collapse. When my sister came down to visit it was always fun to watch her hit the Wall. On the way in from the airport in Gainesville she'd be chattering with manic energy – insisting we stop at the farmer's stand near the 301 to buy strawberries or collard greens, asking for news about the neighbors, observing changes in the scene going by the car window. Then, half an hour after arriving at the house, I'd look over and see her stretched out on the porch sofa, her lips parted, head back, as if chloroformed, wiped out by the sheer nothingness, the silence.

The sounds I associate with Florida used to be: the whistle of the train from Palatka that ran through town at night on its way to Atlanta; the squirrels and raccoons running across the roof as I lay in my bed waiting to fall asleep; my parents breathing in their beds across the hall; and – that most Florida of all sounds – the drone of a small plane crossing the sky in the middle of the afternoon. But only two of these were left after my parents died and the train tracks were torn up and converted to an asphalt trail on which people can now walk and bicycle all the way to Palatka – theoretically.

Palatka is forty minutes' drive to the east; Gainesville, half an hour to the west. Palatka is an old town on the St Johns River that for some reason has remained pretty much the way it always was. Gainesville has not. Gainesville is the main thing, the Paris, the Athens, of North Central Florida. That's because it's the home of the University of Florida, and used to have a wonderful bookstore, and still has gyms and an excellent public library. That's the reason one goes to Gainesville: to get a book you can't find anywhere else. The other reason is to see a doctor: the dermatologists, dentists, ophthalmologists, orthopedists and audiologists who make Gainesville a boomtown in the American medical-industrial complex. Its hospitals are huge and state-of-the-art; Gainesville is where the astronauts are sent if anything goes wrong. Gainesville is the place you go to get your taxes done, eyes examined, teeth cleaned, skin checked. Gainesville is the planet to whose gravitational pull people in the small towns around it are all subject. It's where we know we'll probably be taken when we die – which is why having to put my mother in a nursing home there, and having to take my father into the hospital the day he had his stroke, seemed like such a defeat. There's no way around it: Gainesville gets you in the end.

There is an adult assisted-living place in this town, but what exactly they offer has never been clear to me. For years I was under the impression that it was like Penney Farms, a retirement community half an hour to the east – where for many years the only people admitted were retired missionaries. But I think that rule has been relaxed, along with so much else about Christianity. A young woman I met at the gym who works there once told me, when I asked what the night shift at Lake of the Palms could possibly be like, that residents get out of bed in the middle of the night thinking they are in their own home and fall. Knowing that there is a night shift at Lake of the Palms makes me think I might go there instead of Gainesville when I need to, though I haven't made the effort to tour the place or make inquiries. As Freud said, nobody believes in his own death. For some reason, one thinks one is going to live forever. In a small town, one thinks that Time is not even passing.

The mother of a friend who grew up in Gainesville used to write the date of purchase on the bottom of everything she bought, and whenever she picked up some object she said it was always a surprise to see how much time had gone by. That can happen anywhere, of course, but it seems to happen more easily in Florida – even though North Florida has four seasons and trees lose their leaves in both spring and fall. Much of this part of Florida, in fact, looks prehistoric. There's a prairie south of Grandin that resembles the painted background the museum in Gainesville uses for its diorama of dinosaurs – a flat, golden plain with pine hammocks breaking up the sea of grass – and in the garden I still find shells that must date back to a time when the ocean covered the state, though we are sixty miles from the sea.

When my father settled here the town was just a faded summer resort for people in Jacksonville, fifty-three miles to the north-east, a place where families sent their children for summer camp so they could swim and waterski. Nobody waterskis anymore; the very idea summons up a vanished America, the one that made movies about mermaids played by Esther Williams, and built Cypress Gardens downstate so that tourists sitting on bleachers could watch human pyramids go by on waterskis holding the rope handle that connected them to the speedboat in one hand and a flag in the other. When my father retired, all the lakes in town were high. People skied at five o'clock, after the daily thunderstorm, when the lake was smooth as glass and every pine tree, including the cones, was reflected on the surface of the motionless dark water. We'd ski from the Big Lake down a chain of smaller lakes that were all connected by narrow channels lined with weeds in which we'd been warned not to fall because they were full of water moccasins. The lakes were so high there was water beneath the pilings of the pier at the public beach, and the pier still looked just like the photograph of it on a postcard in the five-and-dime store uptown.

The only other postcards they sold in 1961 showed a woman standing in a bikini beside an alligator with its jaws wide open, and a more generic card that was used for California as well as Florida that featured a little old lady in a lawn chair surrounded by strapping young men in red Speedos above the phrase 'Having the time of my life!'

There was something forlorn and faded even then, however, about the pier at the public beach, the paint peeling off the walls, the concrete shuffleboard court half covered with sand, the moss hanging from the live oaks through which one glimpsed the lake. It looked like a set for the Moon Lake Casino – the one where Blanche's husband shoots himself in *A Streetcar Named Desire* after she discovers his sexual secret.

I hated having to go back down to Florida for Christmas – especially after leaving school and starting life on my own. What was I going back to? A drive-in movie theater whose last movie before it closed was *Lawrence of Arabia*; a grocery store with two refrigerated cases filled with ice-cream sandwiches, its concrete floor strewn with sand; an old clapboard inn that had been gutted by a fire; a decrepit pier on pilings above a receding lake; a grid of sandy streets on which some people from Pennsylvania had built small stucco houses when they founded the community in the 1920s. There was nothing to do at night but lie in bed reading while listening for the whistle of the old freight train, the dog barking down the street, the squirrels and raccoons racing across the roof, the sound of my parents breathing across the hall that made me think of the ship my mother had taken me on when we traveled to New York, when she lay on the bunk bed beneath mine, telling me that the way to fall asleep was to relax my entire body, starting with my fingers and toes. Unfortunately, we were not on a ship in the middle of the ocean – though I might as well have been. Ten years after my parents had retired, I was the only person my age on our street who had not moved away and married. I was the only member of my generation walking out in a navy-blue cashmere sweater with his father's scalloped potatoes to the community park where the neighbors gathered a few days before Christmas to build a bonfire and share a meal. The reason was simple: I was not about to marry and start a family of my own.

Years later the daughter of a neighbor who'd flown to Florida from San Francisco to take care of her dying father, a retired air-conditioning salesman who lived across the street from us and who had prostate cancer, remarked to me with breezy nonchalance as we took a walk one day, 'Everybody here knows you're gay, you know.' Gee, no, I wanted to say, I didn't. But I went on pretending anyway. Walking out with my father's casserole to the Christmas party, I was still the dutiful son, unlike all the other boys my age on that street who'd moved away and already started families of their own. Having to return at Christmas – which is, after all, the celebration of a baby – made me so depressed that I tried thinking up excuses that would absolve me from having to make the trip, anything that got me out of going back to Florida, which felt, for so many reasons, so much like returning to a prison that it seemed right that the actual penitentiary in which the serial killer Ted Bundy was incarcerated was just twenty miles away.

By that point I'd stopped trying to lighten the drive home from the airport with my father with conversation. We simply drove in silence. I even began taking a bus from Jacksonville to Starke to reduce the distance he had to drive to pick me up – till Greyhound discontinued the route. One thing remained the same, however. The boredom of the place had made of my mother such a devotee of television that I knew she would not come out to greet me if my arrival coincided with a dramatic moment on *Donahue*.

There was never a fire in the fireplace when it got cold, because when we tried to have one the living room filled up with smoke. But it was very pleasant in December – the reason, I suppose, for Florida's popularity. But it was not just that; it was good to be home. The scent that greeted me when I walked into the house at Christmastime, a mélange of the Pine-Sol and lemon Pledge the cleaning lady used every other week on the furniture, warmed my heart; the gleam of white terrazzo floors, the comfort of the house. By Christmas the camellias my father planted were in bloom, the kumquat covered with bright golden fruit, the poinsettias red, the lake a silver-blue. The camellias that fell from the bough decomposed on the ground in the same shape they had on the branch, while in the sky above, the fantail of a jet caught the last rays of sunset, a sunset so luminous the bands of color seemed to be submerged beneath a layer of ice. At night the slender scimitar of a new moon floated high above the live oaks, and as I lay in bed listening to the freight train rumbling through town I wondered how I could ever have not wanted to come back.

Nevertheless, the fact that for many years I was still carrying the casserole to the Christmas party in my cashmere sweater, the only unmarried child my age on that street turning up each year, was a source of deep embarrassment. The communal cheer the neighbors exuded, standing around the bonfire in the cold night, with whiskey and beer in hand, all of them part of the Great Chain of Being, made me feel like a fraud. I had nothing in common with them; I was not going to reproduce. I had stopped wearing a suit and tie to church, but after Mass nothing had changed: my mother stood on the steps talking to people, while I fled to the airless car.

After Christmas a wonderful peace descended on the town; the humiliation of the annual Christmas party was behind me. No one ever asked how long I was going to stay. In New York I was still working as an office temp, typing up reports on American attitudes toward Speedo bathing suits at ad agencies or proofreading loan agreements at law firms in Midtown office buildings late at night – there was no reason to go back to Manhattan. That way I witnessed the other seasons. In March the yard turned into a coral reef composed entirely of azaleas, camellias and dogwood. In April the reef crumbled into a fine white dust that settled on the hedge like talcum powder after a car went down our dirt road. In May every Wednesday the widow across the street who brought us a tin of homemade rum balls at Christmas waited in a green pantsuit outside her house to be picked up for bridge at the Women's Club by her best friend. Then, just when everything was so parched that even the azaleas had started to droop, there was the sound of thunder and the daily monsoon arrived.

M y parents had long since traded in their convertible – too jaunty, too young – for a Chevrolet Caprice so big one could have hung a chandelier from the roof. Trips to Chicago shrank to trips to the grocery store and the golf course on the edge of town. Florida was where they lived, where I kept coming back, though nobody asked me questions anymore about what I was doing. One day, when I was sitting in the back seat of the car as we were waiting for a railroad train to go by on our way to the mall, my mother turned back to me and said, apropos of something I forget, 'You are a separate person, you know,' but I felt I wasn't. I couldn't get away from them, which is why I kept coming back to Florida. ∎

TAO RUSPOLI
2020

BEING-IN-THE-WORLD

Geoff Dyer

In October 2019 my wife and I went to the Disney Hall to hear members of the LA Phil play Beethoven's string quartet, op. 132. I put it like that because rather than an established quartet this was just four players from the orchestra. It was OK – which is to say it was also inadequate. They weren't able to generate enough resistance to the leaving-everything-behind soul of the third movement, the 'Heiliger Dankgesang'. The regret at leaving – the reluctance – has to be immense in order to enhance the achieved leave-taking. So it ended up being just an amazing piece of music, finely played, when it has to become so much more. That, in a way, is what it's about; leaving even music itself behind . . . Certainly that's how these late quartets struck Beethoven's contemporaries. There's something there, one of them remarked, as if peering dimly at another world through an inadequate telescope, but we don't know what.

But the above formulation, about leaving music behind, was incomplete. The goal was to leave music behind while still being music. ('Nothing transcends,' Adorno reminds us, 'without that which it transcends.') For Beethoven what greater repose could there have been?

All of this was in my mind during the concert – a sure sign of not being completely transported by it – because I'd spent the weekend at my friend Tao's place in Joshua Tree. I drove out there with Jamie, a laid-back, broad-shouldered surfer. Half the population of Southern California surfs but Jamie had been a pro. He's in his mid-fifties now: the Cliff Booth, we agreed, to my Rick Dalton. I didn't just like hanging out with him; I also felt a kind of pride at having such a dudely friend, as if I became cooler by association. We were dressed almost identically – skateboard shoes, jeans, plaid flannel shirts – and it was easy to forget, as we sat side by side in his clapped-out station wagon, that rather than making me seem cool, those wide, easy-going shoulders of his made me look even scrawnier and more uptight than usual.

On pre-Covid Friday afternoons it often felt as if California was so jammed with cars that it was impossible for anyone to get anywhere until Saturday morning. We were in the car for ages, stuck in traffic for hours in LA and then for hours more in Riverside. It was a relief to get to Tao's but it's intimidating turning up at a place where people are already lounging round the pool or soaking in the hot tub, especially when they are all naked, some are already tripping, and, on one of the loungers, there is a water-wrinkled copy of *Being-in-the-World*, Hubert Dreyfus's commentary on Heidegger.

I'd warned Jamie about this, about the initial intimidation factor, and I'd also told him that while every weekend at Tao's place was guaranteed to be wonderful, each weekend had its own distinctive and unpredictable character of wonderfulness. The previous time I was there I'd held a human brain in my hands (a visiting neuroscientist happened to have one in the trunk of his car). This weekend came to be defined by DMT, something I'd been very keen to try twenty years earlier during my last phase of psychedelic experimentation.

There was some doubt about how best to ingest it. All we had was a little pot pipe. Tao said we needed to mix the DMT with tobacco but I knew, from the few times I'd attempted to smoke hash mixed with tobacco, that this would make me nauseous. In the end we settled for sage instead of tobacco. In every other respect our preparations were meticulous. A comfortable chair was set up facing a dull brown mandala from Bhutan in the living room – home to Tao's superb McIntosh sound system. One person would hold the pipe for whoever was doing the DMT and would then leave, rejoining the others waiting in the kitchen. On the Friday night I sat down comfortably in front of the mandala. The music on the stereo was by SUSS: ambient country, open-sky soundscapes. I took a scorching hit on the pipe, held the smoke in, and then took another, holding it in for only a short time before coughing. I felt a brief inner turbulence and then the mandala glowed a radiant gold and became infinitely three-dimensional. But I always knew exactly where I was and who I was and was fully conscious of the passage of time. Everyone else had similar experiences.

I had another go on Saturday morning and the effects were milder than the night before so three of us – Jamie, me and our friend Danny – set out to buy the correct equipment. This meant, not to put too fine a point on it, buying a crack pipe – easy to do in Joshua Tree as long as you did the polite thing and asked for a glass pipe. After buying the glass pipe that was really a crack pipe that was really a DMT pipe we had an epic breakfast at the Crossroads Cafe, where, as we waited for a table, I received a text from a friend in Dublin. 'This is of the utmost importance: go all the way with a breakthrough dose. Otherwise you won't get what makes it unique.'

For some reason, in addition to a huge egg breakfast each, we had also ordered an enormous helping of pancakes which Danny proceeded to divide up with his fork. Because he had what looked, relatively speaking, like a pancake-sized cold sore on his lip neither Jamie nor I wanted our share of this shared item so Danny set about methodically scarfing the lot. It was such a massive undertaking that Jamie asked if he had 'ever eaten competitively?' This was probably the most unusual question I had ever heard anyone ask and although I had not included questions of any kind in my list of things that might make a weekend at Tao's wonderful this was one of the details that contributed to the wonderfulness of this particular weekend. It's also important to mention that we always refer to Danny as Crop-Top Danny because he wears these crop tops to show off his impressively muscled abdomen, which showed no signs of expansion even after he'd worked his way through both his own breakfast and the bonus pile of pancakes.

We drove back to Tao's in Danny's car, a Buick LeSabre from the 1980s, moving surprisingly fast over the ruts, craters and boulders on the dirt road up to the compound. The car had amazing suspension – though by the time I returned a month later it was out of action, because of a problem with the suspension, which, for all we know, might have been put under additional strain by the quantity of food Danny had snaked away.

To make sure everything would be done properly we watched public-spirited instructional DMT videos on YouTube. There are a lot, some featuring teenagers in their bedrooms, most hosted by older, more experienced heads, at least one of whom looked like he was still recovering from the trauma of Jerry Garcia's passing. A scrupulous evangelist said we needed scales to measure out a fifty-milligram dose. We didn't have scales so we cleverly crushed a two-hundred-milligram ibuprofen pill and divided it into four piles so we'd know roughly what fifty milligrams looked like. The rest of the afternoon was spent hiking up a nearby hill, charging down it again – which I managed to do without twisting my ankle – and hanging out by the pool and hot tub. I was wearing shorts and a faded T-shirt from a bicycle cafe in Sedona. A new couple arrived, at the same time that we had the day before. I expected to be able to enjoy their slight self-consciousness but they felt immediately at ease and were naked in the hot tub within minutes of arriving, leaving me feeling so self-conscious in my T-shirt and shorts that I 'read' *Being-in-the-World*, conscious that I couldn't understand any of it, before getting up to fiddle with the sound system.

For the Saturday night DMT session the living room had been even more beautifully prepared. To one side of the mandala there were lush plants, with a cuddly toy propped up beside them. In *The Celestial Hunter* Roberto Calasso writes of a time when you never knew if an animal you saw might be a god. Looking back it seems clear that this adorable cuddly toy was a god, even though I can't remember which animal it was supposed to be. A cool friend of Tao's who lived nearby had come for dinner: a musician in her mid-thirties, called Janie, confusingly. The identity borders built around these neighbourly consonants proved too porous to be effective; several times in the course of what turned into a long evening I said Janie when I meant Jamie, and Jamie when I meant Janie, as though, along with everything else going on, they were turning into each other. Janie took the first hit of the properly administered DMT and reported very mild effects. Then it was my turn. The experience was even more diluted than it had been in the morning (which had itself been a diminution of what had happened the night before). Surfer Jamie: ditto. Had the DMT gone off? The well-fed Danny went next, lighting the pipe himself. Having broken through multiple times before he was well-placed to deliver a definitive verdict. It works, he said when he came back into the kitchen, but not as powerfully as some he'd taken before. He'd had to breathe his way into it.

By now, after all these failures and false starts, there was only one dose left. I didn't want to do it and neither did Jamie, though our demurral had nothing to do with Danny's cold sore, which, we had learned, was not a cold sore. We had suddenly gone from shortage to surplus. Janie duly stepped up for her second attempt, with Tao lighting the pipe for her. Peeping round the kitchen door we saw her flop back into her seat, as is supposed to happen, watched over by the little cuddly toy-god. Then we heard her groaning.

'She's really far gone,' Tao said.

The groans and moans continued. We became a little concerned, then scared. I was in an entirely characteristic state of mind, balanced between relief ('Thank god it's not me') and regret ('That could have been me'), which encapsulates in miniature much of my experience of being-and-not-being in the world.

After twenty minutes Janie came floating back into the kitchen looking like she'd spent hours, maybe even years, having the best sex of her life, possibly of anyone's life. And she had not been scared at all – which was quite impressive since, by most accounts, DMT is scary.

Even experienced users get scared because it's so far out. You may have been there before but the strangeness of the DMT world is overwhelming. Every time you get there it's as if for the first time – even if, as is commonly reported, it also feels as if you are returning home.

After returning home, having failed to break through to that other home, I spent many hours in the following days watching videos of Terence McKenna, who, in one of them, says the risk with DMT is that you might die of amazement. So it's insane not to try it. We spend a lot of time and money going to the Galápagos; we endure all sorts of inconvenience and discomfort travelling to Sossusvlei in Namibia – and here is a wholly other world you can get to in about fifteen seconds and back from in fifteen minutes, for about fifteen dollars, without leaving your armchair. In another of his videos McKenna says that if a flying saucer landed on the lawn of the White House, DMT would still be the most extraordinary thing in the universe. Even if it goes horribly wrong fifteen minutes is nothing – especially compared with the awful marathon of an acid trip with all its potential for unexpected hazards. The problem is that while, from the point of view of people waiting in the kitchen, you're only gone for as long as it takes to drink a cup of chamomile tea, for the person in the DMT world there is no time. You're stranded in eternity – and a little bit of eternity goes an awful long way. You're stuck you don't know where for fifteen minutes of forever – and you don't know who you are either. Tao forwarded an account by another friend of his, a Heidegger expert, who had tried DMT (under Tao's supervision) and had found it absolutely terrifying. The music he chose to accompany him on this journey into the unknown was not a soothing ambient composition but a late Beethoven quartet (he didn't specify which, unfortunately). That was asking for trouble in multiple ways. You don't want music that demands concentration. You want to create a nice environment, not, as is the case with acid, in order to immerse yourself in it more completely, but in order to settle your nerves before leaving it behind.

So, as everyone says, it is natural to be apprehensive, anxious, afraid. The key thing is to keep breathing, to remain calm, to go with it.

The worse thing is to try to resist because, after that second or third scalding intake of smoke, whatever is going to happen is going to happen anyway. If you're used to meditating, are familiar with breath control, then you can increase the chances of transforming a potential white-knuckle ride into a high-speed glide into this other world. They're all breathers, these Californians: breathers, polyamorous meditators and doers of yoga, whereas I was just a breather in the normal, untutored English sense that I had managed to keep doing it, without thought or discipline, for over sixty years, though there was a time, I remembered from my childhood, when my mother told relatives that I held my breath – it was a quite common thing among kids back then, a stripped-down and instinctive protest against the terms and municipal conditions of being in the world.

It's telling that the two most hesitant people were also the oldest, Jamie and me. At forty I'd have gone for it with abandon and that very abandonment would have increased the chances of everything working out OK. It's not just physical flexibility you lose as you get older, it's also mental. The friend who'd texted me with that message of 'the utmost importance' is thirty-five. Like someone who's listened to the ancient mariner droning on for forty years I'm wiser now than when I first took acid in my early twenties, but what is the point of wisdom, of having ploughed through eleven hundred pages of *Black Lamb and Grey Falcon*, twice, if it reduces the chances of having the breakthrough experience of DMT even once? Isn't that the opposite of wisdom, isn't it uniquely stupid? Especially since, as far as I can discover, DMT, unlike LSD, carries no risk of permanent mental damage or derangement (once you re-emerge from the ultimate permanence of eternity) aside from becoming a bit of a DMT bore. And I have less to lose, now that the brain has done the bulk of the work of which it was ever going to be capable. I expect to live beyond seventy but if we translate the old three-score-years and ten of life expectancy into days of the week then it's now early Sunday morning. Or, if eighty is the new seventy, it's Sunday with a bank holiday Monday thrown in as a bonus day – one of those English bank holidays from the 1970s when everywhere was shut, there was nothing to do, and, for that reason, you'd treat the Sunday night as a Saturday and spend the extra Monday flopping around the house incapacitated by a thumping hangover.

In some ways then the DMT experience is a test. Of one's self. And the result depends on one's ability to lose that self, to leave it behind for ten minutes *and* – the echo of Nietzsche is inevitable – for all of eternity.

The DMT realm: to know it's waiting there, 'pre-formed', as my Dublin friend explained in another text: 'an entirely robust and intact freestanding dimension'. It's reassuring, to know that it's not going anywhere any time soon, that there's still time. That's what enables one to put off going there, to wait for another chance to break on through. ∎

CONTRIBUTORS

Jason Allen-Paisant is a Jamaican poet and non-fiction writer based in the UK. He is also an Associate Professor in Aesthetic Theory at the University of Leeds.

William Atkins' *The Immeasurable World* won the 2019 Stanford Dolman Travel Book of the Year award; his new book, *Exiles*, will be published by Faber in May 2022.

Kevin Childs is a writer and lecturer on culture and art history in the United Kingdom and Italy, where he leads specialised tours of Rome, Venice and Florence. He writes regularly for the *Independent* and the *Huffington Post*, and has also written articles and reviews for the *New Statesman* and *The Times*.

Geoff Dyer is the author of ten non-fiction books and four novels, including *Out of Sheer Rage*, *Zona* and, most recently, *See/Saw*. A fellow of the Royal Society of Literature and a member of the American Academy of Arts and Sciences, Dyer lives in Los Angeles. 'Being-in-the-World' is an extract from *The Last Days of Roger Federer*, forthcoming from Canongate on 9 June 2022, and from Farrar, Straus and Giroux in the US.

Nicole R. Fleetwood is a writer, curator and the James Weldon Johnson Professor at NYU. She is a MacArthur Fellow and the author and curator of *Marking Time: Art in the Age of Mass Incarceration*.

Alex Fleming is a literary translator from Russian and Swedish. Her translations include works by Maxim Osipov, Katrine Marçal and Camilla Sten, and have featured in *Asymptote*, *Litro* and *Image Journal*. She is the editor of *Swedish Book Review*.

Adam Foulds is a poet and novelist. He was named one of *Granta*'s Best of Young British Novelists in 2013 and the Poetry Society's Next Generation Poets in 2014. In 2009 he was made a Fellow of the Royal Society of Literature. His most recent novel, *Dream Sequence*, was published in 2019.

Andrew Holleran is the author of the novels *Dancer from the Dance*, *Nights in Aruba* and *The Beauty of Men*; a book of essays, *Ground Zero*; a collection of short stories, *In September, the Light Changes*; and a novella, *Grief*. 'The Kingdom of Sand' is an extract from his novel of the same title, forthcoming with Farrar, Straus and Giroux in the US and Jonathan Cape in the UK.

Lars Horn holds MAs from the University of Edinburgh; the École normale supérieure, Paris; and Concordia University, Montreal. Horn's work has appeared in the *Kenyon Review*, *Write Across Canada* and *New Writing Scotland*. They live in Miami.

Ishion Hutchinson was born in Port Antonio, Jamaica. He is the author of two books of poetry and the forthcoming book of essays, *Fugitive Tilts*.

Esther Kinsky is a German-born poet, writer, photographer and literary translator. She is the author of seven prose books and seven books of poetry. Her most recent publication in English is *Grove*, translated by Caroline Schmidt.

Megan McDowell is the recipient of a 2020 Award in Literature from the American Academy of Arts and Letters, among other awards, and has been short- or longlisted four times for the International Booker Prize. She lives in Santiago, Chile.

Maxim Osipov has published short stories, novellas, essays and plays, and has won a number of literary prizes. His work has been translated into more than a dozen languages. 'An English Opening' is an extract from the story 'Pieces on a Plane' from *Kilometer 101*, edited by Boris Dralyuk, translated by Boris Dralyuk, Nicolas Pasternak Slater and Alex Fleming, and forthcoming in October from NYRB Classics.

Phalonne Pierre Louis is a Haitian photographer and director, currently working on her first documentary feature film *Sere bouboun*. She works on creative film and video as a camera operator and director of photography.

She is the vice president of the KIT association and a member of FotoKonbit.

Raphaela Rosella is an Australian artist working across socially engaged art and long-form documentary practice. Her work has featured at the Photoquai Photo Biennale and the Noorderlicht Photo Festival. 'The Right to Intimacy' was co-created by Rosella alongside Dayannah, Gillianne, Kayla, Laurinda, Mimi, Nunjul, Rowrow, Tammara, Tricia and their families.

Muhammad Salah is a Sudanese photographer and a visual storyteller based between Berlin and Khartoum, Sudan. His work has been published in the *Washington Post*, the *Guardian* and *Port* magazine.

Rebecca Sollom is an Australian writer living in the UK. She holds a PhD in cosmology from Cambridge and is a recent graduate of UEA's MA in prose fiction. 'National Dress' is an extract from a longer work of the same title.

Alejandro Zambra is the author of the novel *Chilean Poet*, and of five previous works of fiction, including *Multiple Choice* and *My Documents*. The recipient of numerous literary prizes and a New York Public Library Cullman Center Fellowship, he was selected in 2010 as one of *Granta*'s Best of Young Spanish-Language Novelists. He lives in Mexico City.